FOR READING IN THE BATH

CATULLE MENDÈS (1841–1909) was a French man of letters and the protégé of Théophile Gautier, whose daughter, Judith, he married, though their relationship did not last long. In 1860 he founded *La Revue fantaisiste*, publishing such authors as Villiers de L'Isle-Adam and Charles Baudelaire. He gained the reputation as a sensualist after his 'Le Roman d'une Nuit,' which appeared in the same review in 1867, was condemned as immoral, and he was sentenced to a month's imprisonment and a fine of 500 francs for publishing it. He wrote voluminously—plays, poetry, essays, novels, and short stories. Friedrich Nietzsche dedicated his *Dionysian-Dithyrambs* to Mendès, celebrating him as "the greatest and first satyr alive today—not just today . . ."

BRIAN STABLEFORD has been publishing fiction and non-fiction for fifty years. His fiction includes a series of "tales of the biotech revolution" and a series of metaphysical fantasies featuring Edgar Poe's Auguste Dupin. He is presently researching a history of French *roman scientifique* from 1700-1939 for Black Coat Press, translating much of the relevant material into English for the first time, and also translates material from the Decadent and Symbolist Movements.

Catulle Mendès

FOR READING IN THE BATH

Translated and with an Introduction by

Brian Stableford

THIS IS A SNUGGLY BOOK

ISBN: 978-1-943813-88-9

CONTENTS

INTRODUCTION

BORN in Bordeaux, Catulle Mendès (1841-1909) came to Paris in 1859 in order to attempt to build a literary career, and was taken under the wing of Théophile Gautier, whose salon remained an important nucleus of the fading Romantic Movement; Mendès became one of the leading proponents of the "Parnassian Movement," launched with the anthology *Le Parnasse contemporain* (1866), which attempted to renew and revitalize it. Before then, however, he had founded a periodical of his own in 1861, the *Revue fantaisiste*, and it was as the editor of that periodical that he began writing brief "fillers" to make up the required page length of the monthly issues, including many fictional "character sketches" of a kind that were later to fill three collections entitled *Monstres parisiens* in the early 1880s.

Mendès' fondness for risqué material was also exhibited in the pages of the *Revue fantaisiste*, and he proved that he was ahead of his time in that regard when his brief verse drama, "Roman de la nuit" [The Romance of the Night] (1861), was prosecuted for obscenity; he was sentenced to a month's imprisonment and fined five hundred francs. In spite of that setback, he soon built himself a successful career as a journalist, playwright and poet. His relationship with Gautier was spoiled, however, when he married the latter's teenage daughter Judith, although the marriage quickly broke down.

The literary marketplace was only just beginning to recover from the effects of the stern censorship introduced under the Second Empire when it was devastated by the economic upheavals following France's catastrophic defeat in the Franco-Prussian War of 1870. It opened up again in the 1880s, however, aided by important advances in the technologies of printing and paper production, which made newspapers and periodicals much cheaper to produce, resulting in a rapid proliferation and fierce competition. Mendès became an editor again, for the short-lived geographical periodical *Le Monde Inconnu* and the longer-lasting bi-weekly *Revue Populaire*, both launched in 1882. The latter's chief stock-in-trade was reprinted serial novels, but required Mendès once again to employ his expertise in supplying fillers of variable length, initially under the pseudonym Jean-qui-Passe. Many were brief anecdotal sketches of contemporary Parisian life, often featuring Jean-qui-Passe's friend Valentin, who remained the hero of many of Mendès short stories long after the author had abandoned the pseudonym.

Mendès soon quit both periodicals, but continued supplying material in the same vein to numerous other outlets, broadening the scope of his fiction vastly in an urgent quest for variation and originality, but always retaining a particular fondness for the ubiquitous Valentin and the many women he pursues ardently, with varying degrees of success. It was in the context of his quest to master the art of writing ultra-short stories useful for filling small gaps in newspaper pages that Mendès developed the work featured in the present collection, *Pour lire au bain* (1888). The expertise stood him on good stead, and he continued to make use of it, as a prolific contributor to *Gil Blas* and *Le Figaro*, and to the weekly literary supplements of *Le Petit Parisien*, *L'Écho de Paris* and *La Lanterne*. His casual fluency and enormous productivity did not aid his literary reputation, but that is a trifle unfair—as judgments of literary reputation routinely are—and there is a definite artistry as well as craftsmanship in the confection of ultra-short stories, which no one else mastered to the same extent as Mendès during the *fin de siècle*, and few have been able to match since.

The risqué aspect of Mendès' work in this vein is bound to seem a trifle mild by today's far more liberal standards, but that is not a disadvantage; there is much to be said for its cavalier subtlety and amiable delicacy, and in its way the work was ground-breaking, helping to pave the way for many of the writers who similarly became expert in filling the short story slots opened up by the newspapers of the era, including Jean Richepin, Léon Bloy, Octave Mirbeau, Remy de Gourmont and Jean de La Vaudère, many of whom exhibited a similar fascination with the teasingly ill-concealed immorality of the late nineteenth-century Parisian *haut monde*, justly considered as a glorious example to the rest of the world, not simply in terms of sexual license and sophistication, but also in the amiable humor of its approaches to both.

The translations were made from the copy of the 1888 Marpon et Flammarion edition reproduced on the Bibliothèque Nationale's *gallica* website.

—Brian Stableford

FOR READING IN THE BATH

ISN'T bath time, for you, exquisite Parisiennes, the most charming hour of all, even more charming than the one . . . ?

In the little room decorated with flowery silk or gilded mats, under the cheerful mirror in the ceiling that gazes at the disorder of scattered skirts, still inflated, black silk stockings hung on the back of a chair and the crumpled chemise whose dear pleats remember, you abandon yourself with swooning delight to the warm embrace of the water; languishing, drifting in a reverie, doubtless made of hopes, and perhaps reminiscences, while an aromatic mist emanates from the bathtub of snowy alabaster or cracked roseate faience, which is like the vaporization of your moist flesh, and intoxicates you with yourself! Eyes half-closed, heart opening, not entirely asleep but entirely dreaming: a slow dream, in which are mingled, in a mist given to them by an ideal distance, the last early morning walk in the Bois, almost a rendezvous, the visit to the dressmaker—how well it suits you, that pale blue plush dress with acacia flowers!— Madame de Soïnoff's ball, where the Princesse truly looked a fright, and the cotillion waltzes, less ceremonious, when the arms grip a little more tightly, when the breath is a little closer, the waltzes that, even when interrupted, leave hands in hands. Sometimes, also, the face of a young man passes through your mind, with smiling lips and eyes that must weep well. What if he were there, the man you love? There, before you, kneeling, holding out his arms, stammering divine, imploring words? In the infinite wellbeing into which your body and soul are melting, a softness advises you to mute consents, the abandonments that close the eyes. Oh, if he were there! You would not flee the amorous water that presses you all over with a single caress. No resistance. The slide into ecstasy. You accept your defeat with all the more pleasant nonchalance because you know full well that it isn't real; your modesty adapts to a chimerical sin, which seems no less sweet; and, tenderly dying, the eyelashes quivering over your extinct pupils, you conclude your long dream, tipping your head back slightly, one hand supported on the rim of the bathtub.

Then, sometimes, after the dream flees, in the repose of the mind overworked by illusion, it would be pleasant to read a book. But what book? They alarm your delicate languor, the brutal novels that drag modern humanity into the daylight, bloody or soiled with mud. The work worthy of being riffled through by your pretty moist fingers ought to be like your reverie, continuing it without distracting it. Not ambitious and long drawn out, but made of very short stories—your chambermaid has already knocked on the door saying "Is Madame ready to get out of the bath? It's necessary that it should be gently vague, slightly sad, and equally tender; worldly, certainly, poetic too; perverse at times, since you are very subtle, more often chaste, because you are in fact very chaste; always amorous! and that mingled with languorous stories are a few funny anecdotes; for the water of the bath, shaken by your laughter, makes a pretty splashing sound against the cracked roseate faïence or the snowy alabaster. But that book, which I would try in vain to write, what poet as feminine as the divine Amarou,[1] whose soul had lived in the bodies of a hundred women, what poet will give it to you, O exquisite Parisiennes, who will soon be springing from the water, scattering bright droplets, pearls for having touched you, tears for having quit you?"

---

1 The reference is to an alleged translation from Sanskrit by A. L. Apudy, published in France in 1831 as *Anthologie erotique d'Amarou.* It's authenticity is dubious.

THE DUEL

MARIETTE AND MARIANNE resolved to settle their quarrel once and for all in a duel to the death. At any rate, their situation was to longer tenable. Since their lover did not want to renounce either one— oh, how I praise him, and how I envy him!—and since they could not resign themselves to too cruel a division, the best thing to do was to have recourse to a bloody conclusion. To Marianne or Mariette the widower of Mariette or Marianne would belong entirely. So be it! It's settled. Weapons? Foils without buttons. The place? This very boudoir, witness to the challenge. And for seconds, the images of the two combatants in the two Venetian mirrors garlanded with white foliage, in which one can see Columbines kissing the masks of Harlequins.

In an instant, they were undressed. Marianne no longer had anything on but her Alençon lace chemise and her pink silk bloomers: Mariette no longer had anything on but her Malines lace chemise and her blue silk bloomers.

En garde!

They looked at one another before crossing blades.

They found one another—shoulders and arms bare, with the firm stir of the cleavage beneath the transparent whiteness—very beautiful and so delightfully seductive.

What! One of them, in an instant, would be an inert, cold form that no kiss would ever cause to shiver again?

Because of their very beauty, rage returned to their hearts; less violent, however, in Marianne, who, in admiring her adversary, had a tenderness in her eyes.

En garde!

The blades clashed; there was a furious, reckless, charming combat. Small feet struck the carpet in pearl slippers; inflations of air exaggerated the charm of bloomers; arms extending, snowy pink, and the panting of heaving breasts . . .

Marianne uttered a cry.

She thought she had seen blood, a drop of blood, on her rival's breast! Without a doubt she had wounded her, perhaps killed her. She dropped her weapon, threw herself upon Mariette, full of repentance, and started to kiss, while weeping, the wound she had inflicted. Perhaps she thought—because of something she remembered reading—that she might cure her victim by sucking blood from her wound! She was all the more borne to believe that because Mariette, now, did not appear to be suffering any pain; she was breathing easily, a little forcefully. One thing, however, surprised Marianne: she did not feel, beneath her lips, the dampness of blood.

She recoiled, looked, and smiled . . .

The wound that she had kissed, protruding through the Malines, was Mariette's nipple.

EMPTY NESTS

THROUGH the window open to the winter sun-light—while a fire was blazing in the hearth—they watched the clouds passing in the sky, slowly and heavily, with the indolence of enormous white beasts that had rolled in the snow and were washing themselves in the azure. The slope of the stream, rippling like pulled satin, was prolonged between the skeletons of the trees of the broad avenue, all the way from the basin, which gave the impression of a slightly inclined thin blue crescent, to the distant hills, where forests of frail branches rose above the mist, making an infinite, vague, cool backcloth; and the flames of the logs, between the curtains, wrapped around them, very closely, the intimate warmth of a boudoir. They were at home, in the presence of all of space. There, all of nature; here, only them.

How beautiful the celestial immensity is, so pure and so diaphanous that one sometimes expects to see trans-parent angels there! How sweet the tender huddling is of two hearts in the caressant narrowness of the beloved room! Little paradises are worth as much as great heavens. Bonjour, God! And they kiss one another on the lips.

But because she pushes the hypocrisy of innocence—naughty girl!—as far as perfect ingenuousness, she sud-denly says, thumping the table: "I want to go hunt for birds' nests in the woods."

He did not object that it was winter, that there were no leaves on the trees or chicks in the nests. He had lost the habit a long time ago, even in thought, of resisting the caprices of the atrocious child; to each of Juliette's caprices, he said: "Monseigneur!"

Soon, muffled in furs, they were running, he following her, along the pale avenue, and when they were in the wood made of black branches rattling in the wind under the cold sun, she searched the brushwood and the low branches for nests, with the leaps and squeals of a little girl.

Nests she found, but devoid of birds, the nests of last spring, in which not so much as a feather remained. She searched again; not a single little finch without down, not a single half-naked warbler shivering and opening its yellow beak.

"Oh, yes," she said, "it's because it's February." Then she added, huddling against him, affectionately, with the air of a child afraid of being beaten: "I'm very stupid, aren't I, and I'm sure you're laughing at me?"

But he replied, with the melancholy of disappointed cherished hopes: "Have I the right to laugh at you, Juliette—I who have waited for such a long time, in vain, for the awakening of the bird of Amour beneath the snow of your empty heart?"

THE GOOD FRIEND

KNOCK! KNOCK!

"What is it?"

"Open the door!"

"At this hour? You can't think so, Monsieur. I'm going to bed; I've just thrown my corset embroidered with pink plush on to the armchair, and I've taken off one of my black silk stockings."

"Let me take off the other one."

"Impertinent! Go on your way."

"I love you."

"I'd rather no one loved me."

"I'm ready to die for you."

"Live, die, what does it matter to me?"

"I'm young."

"And naïve. Go away."

"I'm handsome."

"And conceited. Go away, I tell you."

"I'm rich."

"And stupid. Go away, or I'll call for help."

"I'm the lover of your friend Clementine."

"Oh! Why didn't you say so sooner?" said the young woman, opening the door.

THE VEIL

VALENTIN spoke to her in a whisper, almost on his knees, in the fiacre, and Juliette, wrapped up in her furs, sensitive to the cold or fearful, moved away, huddled in the corner, troubled by the hands that followed her hands or, more craftily, beneath the unfastened cloak, pretended not to be seeking and finding—the innocent hypocrisy of chance—one of the buttons of her bodice, a roundel of cornelian or silk, which slipped and, scarcely touched, emerged so swiftly from its buttonhole, without one even thinking about it!

Through her thick veil and the window blanched by the mist of breath, Juliette gazed intently at the long line of fortifications looming up, verdantly, as if the plain were arching its back, while Valentin asked for everything from the woman who, alas, gave him nothing. Gradually, however, she softened, the naughty girl, and, without too much difficulty, she condescended to let him snatch a kiss on one of her eyelids. But only one, only on one, and, moreover, with a firmness that could not be denied, she stipulated that he had to take that kiss through the veil.

He accepted that cruel condition, perhaps hoping for the delights praised by one of the most charming verses of François Coppée.

Then, resigned, she closed her eyes. What had she to fear? The thickness of the lace, over the closed eyelid, would intercept the warmth of overexcited lips; the snowy modesty of her skin would not know the mouth, the mouth that devours and burns.

It was the left eye that he chose! He kissed it tenderly, at length, believing that all its stellar radiance would reach the lips, and enter into the heart.

But Juliette was astonished to be troubled. How could it be that she felt the warm pressure so closely, so immediately? She was quite sure that the veil had not been lifted, since she had its tremulous caress on her cheek. She became increasingly troubled, penetrated by tenderness, invaded by languor. A desire came to her that the kiss should be long, longer, even longer . . .

Her arms, slowly raised with the possibility of an embrace, fell back . . .

Frightened, she pushed Valentine away and put her hand to the place of the kiss. She uttered a cry of anger and shame, for she felt, beneath her finger, the naked eyelid, still slightly damp from the slow caress.

Valentin, faithful to his promise, had not raised the veil, but before the kiss, with a single bite, he had ripped, sucked in and swallowed the fragment of lace that defended and hid the dear little star.

THE GOOD RESOLUTION

WELL, yes, her resolution was made! She would go to the rendezvous, she would commit the signal folly—her, a great and perfectly virtuous lady—of going to ring the doorbell of a bachelor apartment and entering, veil raised, into the boudoir-cum-smoking room where the perfume of Havanas would be softened by musk exhaled by frivolous visitors, or perhaps trailing from the black velvet mask of Mademoiselle Anatoline Meyer of the Nouveautés, forgotten there after the last Opéra ball.

It would be a great imprudence, without a doubt! No matter, since her intentions were absolutely pure. The sentiment of duty was dictating her conduct. She judged it necessary, and truly worthy of her, to give a lesson to the impertinent fellow who, the previous evening, during a waltz, had dared to whisper in her ear in a tremulous voice: "You'll come, won't you?"

What did he hope for, the conceited fellow? He had only been rendering his cares for six months; they were only at the stage of mild flirtations of fingers that quit one another slowly, gazes that only half-turned away, and he suddenly risked that brutal and ludicrous extremity? Did he think, then, that as soon as she arrived, he would only have to put his arms around her and carry her away, bewildered by tenderness, her arms devoid of strength and her eyes dazed beneath lashes moistened by tears? A fine opinion he had of her, in truth.

Married for less than two years, still only experiencing for her husband a very tolerable distaste, having victoriously rejected the enterprises of the most passionate and the most adroit suitors, she was irreproachable, thank God, and worthy of every respect. She would punish the insolent fellow, with an exemplary punishment; she would enter his apartment calmly, coolly, and with great dignity—to be dignified might perhaps be difficult, because of his fleshy pink lips that always wanted to smile and his warm brown eyes that had the devil in their pupils, but she would try anyway—she would go into his apartment with her head held high, speaking gravely.

"Yes, Monsieur, I've come, because I didn't want to give you the conceit of thinking that I was afraid of you. I offer myself to danger because I scorn it. And I've also come to tell you my sentiment regarding your conduct. It is unworthy of a gentleman. I am an honest woman, sincerely and loyally attached to my duties. In the family whose illustrious name I quit for an equally glorious name, I received an austere education, I had noble examples before my eyes.

"If my grandmother was reproached for having mounted a horse behind a Cossack officer in 1815, it is because she was calumniated by liberals and republicans. The women of my family, when they mounted a horse, did so with the propriety that is the distinctive characteristic of all their actions. One of my ancestresses was at Fontenoy, dressed as a man, and such was the restraint of her heroic mores that no one ever attempted to discover whether she was a woman! It's true that she was ugly. As for me, I'm her worthy descendant for virtue, if not for ugliness, for one can't be perfect.

"I intend, amid the laxity of modern mores, to keep intact an honor that goes back ten centuries. You are despicable, Monsieur! You thought you had encountered one of those creatures devoid of strength of mind—all too frequent, alas!—who let themselves drift with the current of passions or caprices. I have enough esteem for you to believe that you will recognize your error, and that after the harsh lesson I have been obliged to give you, you will abandon, in a definitive fashion, culpable hopes that are insults to me."

Yes, she would say that, and other things too, serenely, firmly and inexorably, and he would not fail to bow down humbly, full of admiration and repentance, convinced.

At any rate, while composing the scenario of her victory in that fashion and preparing her speech, the adorable young woman began to get dressed—for the hour of the rendezvous was approaching—and after having put on black fishnet stockings through which the skin showed through in droplets of pink milk, and the Valenciennes chemise that put a cloud of snowy mist over her nudity, she chose light diaphanous silk bloomers from the mirror-fronted cupboard, decorated with lace, which were only fastened at the hip by a single button.

THE VILLAGE MARDI GRAS

JULIETTE had said to him, between two doors, while the serious people were playing whist in the drawing room: "Tomorrow, Tuesday, I shall be at my great-uncle's house in Villemomble. Since you say that you love me, and since you have this folly of not being able to spend a day without seeing me, go to Villemomble yourself tomorrow. Walk along the single street, under my great-uncle's windows. The house is next-door to a draper's shop. Walk patiently. At noon or thereabouts, I'll open the casement and smile at you from a distance. A smile is a great deal more than you deserve."

It was more than he had ever dared to desire.

The next day, well before noon, he was in the main street of Villemomble, pacing back and forth, gazing passionately at the window where Juliette would appear. An exceedingly cold wind was stinging his face, tousling his hair, throwing damp dust and grit all over him. He did not care about the wind; he would have braved cyclones.

What can it matter if a cloud in the air
Hurls tempests and lightning as it passes by?

Was he not going to see her in a moment, there, above him, smiling? The mere hope of that smile—for she had the teeth of a little cat that bites!—would repay him for the tedium of waiting, and he loved the grit that was tearing his skin. He was still marching past the houses, expectantly. Passers-by considered him with surprise. In order to put on a show he stopped in front of the draper's window, where, because of the carnival, costumes had been put on display of stevedores, Alpine shepherdesses and clowns, eye-masks of fringed satin, grotesque face masks and enormous false noses. Doubtless some ball would be held in the hundred-seater drawing room of the pastry-maker of Villemomble.

He gazed at the carnival display with an interested expression—but very anxious, for noon had just chimed and Juliette had not shown herself. Oh, that closed window! But Juliette had told him to be patient. He was still gazing—or making a semblance of gazing—at the false noses, the masks and the disguises. He finally perceived the shopkeepers looking at him suspiciously. What was that stranger doing peering into the shop window like that and not coming in, not buying anything, not hiring anything? He dreaded that he might give people ideas, might compromise Juliette.

In order to justify his presence, he opened the door and, after hesitating between various objects, ended up by choosing—while thinking about Juliette's pretty pink nose and the promised smile—a gigantic and extraordinary nose of painted cardboard: a red, sky blue and apple green nose, on which colossal warts blossomed comically, a nose before which the criers of the carnival guffawed. He carried away his purchase wrapped in newspaper and resumed pacing back and forth.

Half past twelve! Had Juliette forgotten, or was she exaggerating her customary cruelty, the coquette, to the extent of refusing him the alms of a smile? While he was going back and forth in the wind, the cardboard nose in the newspaper, shaken and torn by the squalls, irritated him singularly. He had a strong desire to throw it into some corner, but he dared not, for fear of being seen. He did not stop walking, patiently.

Finally, finally! He was not mistaken: the curtain of a window had stirred; a quiver of the catch announced that it was about to open. A few seconds more and he would see Juliette's smile, such a pretty smile, so tender, which would put the delights of paradise into his soul. He extended his arms recklessly.

Juliette did, indeed, appear. But she did not limit herself to smiling; scarcely had she leaned on her windowsill than she was gripped by mad laughter, ever-increasing and inextinguishable: a cruel laughter, mocking and humiliating.

Stupefied, he put his hands to his face instinctively, and realized, poor fellow, that, not knowing what he was doing, without thinking about it, he had put on his own nose, the enormous red, sky blue and apple green carnival nose.

BURNING WATER

AS he had a fever, the cruel fever of amour, he resolved, the poor amorous fellow, to go and bathe in
the stream, so cool and so calm, that flowed over shiny
pebbles.

Someone had said to him: "Since you're suffering,
without respite and without hope, since you have in
your heart, on your brow and on your lips the heat of
eternally disappointed desire, you need to go into that
water and remain there for a long time, for since time
immemorial it has had the virtue of extinguishing the
conflagrations of passion; and many who were no less
ill than you have found it very soothing. Anyone in the
region can tell you that."

He therefore let himself slide from the bank into the
stream. But scarcely had he descended into the freshness
of the water than he felt over his entire body, something
like the grip of embers, an envelope of flame. He fled
across the fields. The universal burn clung to his skin,
devouring it and consuming it. He had never been sub-
jected to such an unbearable torture.

When he complained about it that evening to the
woman who did not love him, she said: "Oh, I know
why. It's because one day, as I was walking beside that
stream, I let one of the little flowers that were in my hair
fall into it."

THE ADVANCE GUARD

THEY both adored him, him alone! An amorous folly with the ruses of caprice and the transports of passion. There were people who affirmed that the adventure would conclude with a duel, an encounter with pistols at twenty paces, or a clash of swords, one morning in a clearing at Meudon. It is certain that Madame de Lurcy-Sevi went to Cain's four times a week, and Madame de Graçay to Ruze's every day.[1]

How could those prudent socialites, always mistresses of themselves, have been overcome by such an excessive fantasy, which troubled their life and disorganized their habits like a gust of wind at a street corner blowing off a maidservant's hat and tousling her hair?

Monsieur de Queyras, undoubtedly, was a man of the world, with an elegant stance, the best tailor in Paris, quite young, with lovely eyes, but the two lovestruck women had seen many other eyes like his smiling and weeping! No matter; it was for him that they were dying of tenderness and being consumed by desire. Was their amour exasperated by their very rivalry? One is inclined

---

1 The fencing-master Adolphe Ruze co-founded Le Jeune Épée in 1891. A fencing-master named Cain is included in a list of the fencing-rooms of Paris in Benjamin Cummings Truman's *The Field of Honor* (1883).

to think that the hypothesis is not improbable. Women readily covet, furiously, what they would scarcely have desired if others had no desire for it. Taking is not always amusing, but stealing is exquisite. They only delight in being queens if they are dethroning someone else. Make a semblance of loving me, Madame, in order that your friend will adore me, and if you give me your hand to kiss, I can aspire to her lips!

Each of the two rivals would have offered anything, yielded anything, in order that the other might offer anything in vain. There was between them, before the duel with pistols or words, a contest of extravagances and audacities. When they had realized that ploys and flirtations had no effect, they resorted to extreme temerities. Who sent enormous bunches of Nice violets to Monsieur de Queyras' house every morning, with a card among the flowers? Madame de Graçay or Madame de Lurcy-Sevi. Who wore ribbons at the Opéra, amid the lace of her bodice, in the colors that Monsieur de Queyras' jockey had worn the day before at Auteuil? Madame de Lurcy-Sevi or Madame de Graçay. Once, one of them waited until four o'clock in the morning at the door of a club, and as four o'clock chimed she uttered a cry of rage: her rival was also waiting at the same door, on foot, in the mud!

Meanwhile, the gentleman to whom so many violent tributes were addressed did not remain impassive; he was hesitating, that's all. Both were equally beautiful, one with her night-black hair, the other with her dawn-blonde hair; before two equally ardent passions, he would not insult them with an absurd division. The sharing could only happen later, over time. He wanted to choose, he

32

owed it to them to choose, to have a preference. But his gratitude for that double amour was so profound that he would have thought himself truly culpable if he had settled on one of the two good fortunes that were offered to him without a veritably serious, determining reason.

Madame de Graçay and Madame de Lurcy-Sevi understood that honest sentiment so well that their unique thought was to divine the proof of devotion or the temptation that would attract the undecided individual toward one or the other of them, and each of them suffered the worst anguish in the fear of being anticipated.

Once, they thought they had divined it—and they had indeed, divined it—because Monsieur de Queyras, during a matinee at the Herz salle, had looked for a long time, with a comparative gaze, at the two rivals' necklines.

The following day, when they entered Madame de Ruremonde's ball together—for they were excellent friends—there was a murmur of astonishment. Never had the tranquil immodesty of the neckline surpassed its limits to such a degree! As white as snow on to which two roses had been cast, Madame de Graçay's breasts were offered almost unveiled, and Madame de Surcy-Levi's, more reminiscent of two oranges, brilliant and slightly gilded, bulbous and stirring, concentrated all their quivering in their warm double roundness.

Monsieur de Queyras gazed.

The moment was supreme. Evidently, the choice, which they could no longer put off without realizing the mythological nudity of goddesses on Maunt Ida, was about to be a fait accompli.

Madame de Lurcy-Sevi considered her rival.

She saw that Madame de Graçay, because of her white amplitude, appeared more décolleté.

She had the courage of ultimate crises.

Pretending to be inconvenienced by the heat of the ballroom, she let herself fall into an armchair; then, before the eyes of Monsieur de Queyras, who hastened forward urgently, she violently snatched away her entire bodice, and fainted, sure of herself.

Monsieur de Queyras bent down, under the guise of picking up her fallen fan, whispering the words of confession.

Afterwards, Madame de Graçay thought to avenge her defeat by saying that it was impossible to battle against an enemy so prompt to unleash the advance guard. But words could do nothing against facts. Last month, at Nice, I, who am writing this for beautiful enamored bathers, saw Monsieur de Queyras and Madame de Lurcy-Sevi walking along the seashore together, very close to one another, whispering ecstatically. She had a very high neckline, as, in general, after a victory, one puts on civilian dress.

JULIETTE VICTORIOUS

JULIETTE had said this to him: "I consent to that! I shall come to your apartment tomorrow. Your apartment. Me, to your apartment! Am I not admirably good? I advise you to fall to your knees immediately, in order to thank me with tears of joy. And it's at lunch time that I shall enter your detestable lodgings, where the Ylang-Ylang of ancient amours should be served. The menu? I only eat crunchy things, in order to give my feline teeth the illusion of the bones of little birds devoured alive, and I've never understood that one can drink anything except Asti Spumante. But if I grant you the signal favor of my presence, Monsieur, it's on one condition."

"What's that?" Valentin had asked.

"By my lips, which are all of the sky, by my lips, which are all roses, by my hair, in which are all perfumes—and also on your faith as a gallant man—you will swear to me that you will not abuse our tête-à-tête in any fashion, not even to kiss the little finger of my glove thrown on the table, nor seek to discover whether, above the elbow, I have a little pink birthmark."

Unshakably resolved not to keep any of his promises, Valentin had consented to all oaths, and that is why, the next day, in the smoking-room upholstered in leather trimmed with gold where the table had been set, next to the blazing logs which made the sun shining through the open window seem pale, Juliette was nibbling crayfish between her redder lips, while a little foam of Asti, like a froth of sap, remained at the corners of her mouth.

At fist, Valentin's conduct was, in truth, worthy of all praise. Not one excessively ardent word or overly keen gaze. Perfect. He did not even try to switch glasses! If he had had a heart of stone—like hers—he could not have shown a more irreproachable reserve. Suddenly, however, without transition, as if the precise moment had come for a long-premeditated accomplishment, he cried: "I adore you!" and took her in his arms.

Frightened, and so beautiful in her undone hair, she struggled desperately, holding on to the curtains of the room, not wanting to fall on to the soft furs on the floor, which made a bed of white foam. With exclamations of hatred and cries of rage or fear, she reproached him for his broken word.

"Perjurer! Wretch! Swine!"

Oh, how sweet you are, frightful words! He was intoxicated by the insults because of the voice, and he clung ever more tightly to Juliette, whose strength and wrath finally weakened. A mildness gradually invaded her, in spite of herself, and she became languid; her eyes softened to a moist tenderness. Her resistance, no longer menacing, asked for mercy.

"Well, yes, I love you! It's true, I love you! I've been a coquette, I've made you suffer. I was wrong, I repent, I love you!"

She would no longer refuse herself, she would submit. She only asked not to be surprised thus, to wait for a few days—not even a few days, until tomorrow. Tomorrow, she would come back, very good and very obedient. He could believe it, she would come back.

But he kept holding her, devoid of confidence.

"So be it!" she murmured, finally, dying under the transport of kisses. "So be it, I'm vanquished, I belong to you, today, forever. But a moment, oh, nothing but a moment, I implore you, give me one . . ."

This time he felt full of an infinite joy. She was giving in, she really wanted it! At the same time, being a practical man, he imagined the reason for the short respite requested. Even abandonment—especially abandonment—must have its coquetry; he glimpsed the necessity of a last dash of rice-powder.

Tenderized by gratitude, dazed by imminent happiness, he loosened his grip, slowly backed away while she blew him a kiss, blushing, and left the room, already almost nuptial, which he would soon reenter. For she was finally his! After so much cruel flirtation, so many refusals and so much bitter waiting, the object of his adoration was softening, and not saying no, saying yes. Surges of joy and pride rose from his triumphant heart to his throat. He would possess her, the exquisite and delicious creature, so white, all luminous, in flower!

A burst of laughter rang out with the sound of a closing door. Oh, horrible suspicion! He ran, traversed the dining room and the antechamber, and arrived on the landing just in time to see Juliette's hat disappear, down below, along the turning staircase, and the burst of laughter rose again in the stairwell, like a panicked bird bumping into the walls of its cage.

MESDEMOISELLES MÉNECHME

TWINS, and identical; as similar as two leaves on the same branch, two drops of the same liquid, two keys on the same piano.

Only one thing—but something very obscure and secret—differentiates the two young sisters: Marthe has never felt her little hand with bright fingernails quiver under amorous lips, whereas Thérèse no longer has anything to offer to a kiss that she has not already offered.

Evening walks, two by two, between male and female cousins are not without peril, especially under arbors scarcely traversed by the moonlight in which there are benches.

However, Thérèse is going to marry, and not the person who offered her his arm in the country, after innocent games.

She is very anxious, Thérèse, and the parents, who have a few suspicions about the excessively prolonged walk, are as anxious as their daughter, for the future husband is not reputed to be a man without experience, and, if he experiences a disappointment, he is quite capable of proclaiming his discontentment the day after the wedding, impolitely.

A chimerical fear! When midday chimes, the husband emerges triumphantly from the nuptial chamber, and he has the air of a victorious knight who has just conquered Eldorado!

The joy of the parents is so great that they no longer give any thought to the long walk under the arbor, and do not hear Thérèse, the new bride, whisper to Marthe: "Thank you, little sister."

THE DEFOLIATED NAME

"FINALLY! Finally!" he cried. "You love me, Juliette! You love me, I know!"

"Eh! Who told you that?" she asked.

"You did—or your name, which is the same thing."

"Are you losing your mind?"

"I'm gaining your heart! Your name itself, your adored name, has made me the confession of the love that you're hiding from me, cruel woman!"

"You're a fool."

"I'm a god."

"Would you care to explain?"

"Right away."

And then he told her about it.

Ingenuous by virtue of tenderness—he was at the age, alas, when illusions return—he had wanted to ask the daisies in the wood whether Juliette loved him. But the Rue Taitbout is a long way from Meudon, where little flowers, in any case, were not yet smiling in the yellow moss. What could he do? An idea occurred to him. Was not the name Juliette as fresh and florid as a daisy? He defoliated the name, petal by petal, no, letter by letter: J, she loves me; u, a little; l, a lot; i, passionately; e, not at all; t, she loves me; t, a little; e, a lot! The only thing that prevented him going mad with joy was that he already was, with amour.

"Monsieur Valentin," said Juliette, with gravity, "you are perfectly ridiculous. I am not a little girl in a provincial suburb who reads novels in secret and wears a blue ribbon in a diagonal cross like Monsieur Scribe's ingénues. I beg you to spare me daisies and other little flowers. I am a serious woman. I am dressed by the best couturiers, and my hats come from an illustrious milliner. I am seen at the premières of all operettas; I have a box at the Opéra and I find Monsieur Saint-Saëns' music very tedious: all in all, a person of taste, and practical, who is not interested in any fashion in childish idylls. Besides which, I beg you to notice one thing: my name is not Juliette; it is you who has given me that name, for the greater convenience of your diminutive rhymes. My real name is Julie, and in consequence, the veritable response is *not at all*!"

THE PORTRAIT

MADAME THÉRÈSE D'ALBEREINE is almost as beautiful as the portrait in which Carolus Duran[1] has represented her white and gold on a red background, with the opulent flow of her russet hair, lips the color of blood, bare shoulders and her cleavage splitting her neckline.

She would even be entirely as beautiful, if she deigned to show herself in the bold costume of the portrait, a cascade of fabric poorly retained by lazy hands, the undress of a socialite playing the bacchante.

But Thérèse d'Albereine is as chaste, in person, as she is the contrary in paint, and the portrait, to which she consented with an unknown intention, the portrait that reveals everything, that undresses her, is hidden from gazes in a distant boudoir.

Pious, even devoted, she fulfills her religious duties firmly, goes to mass, confesses, takes communion. Very austere, a grave visage, a cold heart and a high neckline. Married, she did not love her husband; widowed, she has no lover, dismissing with an astonished smile and a gesture that irritates overly tender urgencies and exaggeratedly

---

1 The portraitist Charles Durand (1837-1917) preferred to sign himself Carolus Duran

respectful salutations that would soon become, if they were allowed to go unchecked, amorous genuflections.

It would be in vain that Chérubin sang his ballad to her; she would kiss the lips of the unconscious Don Juan after the shipwreck without any disturbance to her heart or her senses; and if Comte Almaviva cooed his serenade beneath her window, she would have a few coins thrown to the passing musician.[1]

She has never lent an ear to the subtle debaucheries that rediscover, in order to instill covetousness and troubling delights, the slow and insinuating voice, scarcely heard and so quickly understood, of the Serpent in the branches; she does not even lament the ingenuous lovers who still believe in defoliated daisies with which they mingle a dew of tears.

Those who have died for love of her sleep in tombs to which she does not know the route; it would not be seemly for her to go to the cemetery, since they are asleep there.

In vain, too, the frantic Damned, devourers of virgins and wives, have sent her bouquets of pale flowers, still moist with the tears of rage of their sleepless nights and warm from having been crushed to their breasts in vain embraces.

She follows her path, untroubled, through desires, amours and tumultuous dreams, as cold Arethusas run through melting snow; she smiles, pushing disdain as far as indulgence.

---

1 The references are to Mozart's opera known in English as *The Marriage of Figaro.*.

But Bertine, the chambermaid, going past one evening, has heard a voice behind the door of the distant boudoir, a voice punctuated by prayers and sobs; and, curious, she has put her eye to the keyhole.

A handsome young man, in a black suit, with a sprig of lilac in his buttonhole, was on his knees before the portrait pained by Carolus Duran, in which Madame d'Albereine is standing, white and gold against a red background, with the opulent flow of her russet hair, lips the color of blood, bare shoulders and her cleavage splitting her neckline.

And that young man, kneeling in dolorous ecstasy, his eyes full of tears, extending his arms toward the magnificent image or striking his breast, was Madame d'Albereine herself, in a black suit with lilac in the buttonhole, who was repeating, breathlessly: "Thérèse, Thérèse, I love you eternally!"

ZUT!

SHE said the nasty little word so prettily! Dainty and precious with her mischievous face and her feline blinking eyes, her fists on her hips, her breasts thrust forward and her bosom heaving, like that of a bird about to sing, she launched it so swiftly and so briskly, that word—oh, the pink bow of her lips!—that it departed like a fletched golden arrow, with a thin hiss of air, and stung. That syllable, young hunter Amour, was the surest dart in your quiver! And because she was not unaware that she said "Zut!" very well, she said "Zut!" very often.

At any moment, to anyone, without any appreciable reason, in a low voice or a loud voice, with the abruptness of a jack-in-the-box and the impertinence of a challenging little laugh, she said "Zut!" showing all her teeth, bright and pretty. But the person to whom she said "Zut!" more frequently than anyone else was the poor fellow by whom she was adored and whom she pretended not to love. When he knelt before her, trembling and submissive, with the raised arms of a weeping supplicant, it was always the wicked word that she laughed in his face, leaning forward slightly, putting her breath on his lips.

Oh, the exquisite and adorable coquette!

"I'm fainting with tenderness and dying of desire!"

"Zut!" she replied.

"I'd give my life to kiss the nail of your little finger!"

"Zut!" she said.

"I shall blow my brains out if you won't deign to love me!"

"Zut!" she said again, leaning a little further forward, and almost brushing him with her pretty pink face, quivering with laughter, in which the lips were a kiss in flower, in which frissons curled the corners like little flames.

He lost patience because of that detestable malignity.

Once, having surprised her in the boudoir of lace and silk at the complicit hour of dusk, he took her in his arms violently and hugged her, resistant, and covered her hair, her forehead, her eyes, her neck and her lips with vengeful caresses. She struggled and writhed, crying out beneath his victorious mouth; he paid no heed to that anger of a bird that one is holding in one's hand and which tries to peck; he held her more tightly, more ardently.

Then, seeing herself near to being vanquished, she renounced the efforts of a vain struggle; she uttered laments and shed tears; she begged for mercy. But he, triumphant, said: "Zut!" in a reckless redoubling of kisses.

HER LIPS

"HER HAIR?" I asked him.

"Her hair?" said Valentin. "It does not resemble the reflections of gold or the radiance of the sun, because gold is cold and the sun is dull; radiant and warm, burning the fingers and burning the eyes, as blonde here as Sauterne, and as yellow there as old Cognac, and twisting further away like fiery snakes, it is an enormous accumulated conflagration, and an imperious intoxication emanates from it so perverse that the Devil must certainly have made that hair—the Devil, the dresser of courtesans and the hairdresser of beautiful young women for the human masquerade—with the flames of his most infernal pyre, the one in which the lustful are punished."

"Her forehead?" I asked him.

"Her forehead?" said Valentin. "It is narrow and pale, reminiscent of a headband of snow that she has placed above her eyebrows in order to cool the rising heat of desires."

"Her nose?" I asked him.

"Her nose?" said Valentin. "I have dedicated this frivolous quatrain to it:

"On her little pink face
Agitating wings of flesh
Her nose perches like a bird.
Impertinent, tail in the air!"

"Her eyes?" I asked him

"Her eyes?" said Valentin. "If one put a drop of diamond into the heart of burning topazes, in which all the gleam of all the stars were slumbering, quintessentialized, the topazes might perhaps resemble her eyes."

"Her cheeks?" I asked him.

"Her cheeks?" said Valentin. "As she is a young woman, and a Parisienne, she adds to the candor of her skin the deceit of perfumery. Naïve and complex, she is fresh and made-up. She has velvet and velveteen. Whoever brushes her cheek believes that he is respiring a wild rose that has been painted."

"And her lips?" I asked him.

Valentin hesitated.

"Her lips?" he said. "I've scarcely seen them."

"You've scarcely seen them?"

"Well, of course," he cried, "since I'm always kissing them!"

UNDER THE OLEANDERS

ONCE, when Duke Theseus was walking with Hippolyta, queen of the Amazons, in a wood near Athens, they saw a young faun under a bush of flowering oleanders on the river bank, who was tickling the nacreous rosy nose of a nymph asleep on the moss with the tip of a perfumed branch.

"Why is that little faun tickling the nose of that sleeping nymph?" asked the Duke.

"Doubtless in order that, having woken up, she can hear him talk about love," said the queen.

But the nymph did not wake up. Her nostrils merely quivered from time to time, under the odorous caress.

The faun decided to employ another means; he made a little basket of his two hands and filled it with flowers, and he allowed all the flowers to fall from a height onto the throat of the sleeping hamadryad. Slowly, with a dreaming arm, the nymph pushed the light burden aside; but she did not wake up.

The faun began to caper around her, rustling the grass, breaking branches; it was like the sound of an entire litter of wolf-cubs quarreling in the undergrowth; but the nymph was still asleep, her marble-pale bosom rising and falling like a milky tide.

The faun clapped his hands, shouted, sang, imitated the voices of the wild beasts or tender birds that showed their irritation or uttered plaints in the wood near Athens; there were lion's roars that Bottom would have envied, doves' cooings that would have melted Lysander's heart; the nymph remained motionless in sleep, like a lily caught in the snow.

Then, the little faun having begun to weep, Duke Theseus took pity on the infant demigod and drew his gleaming sword, which he had so soften resounded on armor in battle; rudely, he struck a nearby rock, which rang terribly in the air; one might have thought that a duel of heroes and gods was racing through the branches, and the echo howled like a wounded warrior! But the eyelids of the hamadryad, a statue fallen in the grass, did not even quiver.

"Someone has hurt her," said the queen of the Amazons.

And she drew nearer to Duke Theseus, and then kissed him, long and ardently, on the lips. At the sound of the kiss, the nymph woke up, and put her charmed arms around the young faun's neck.

IN THE TWENTY-FIRST CENTURY

IT is time for the tour of the lake. The two adorable spouses, lying on the cushions of the carriage, wrap themselves in furs, and Laure's hair is all golden, and Jane's hair is ebony-blue like a raven's wing, in the cool light of the winter sun. They have not been seen for a long time—three whole months. After the beautiful day of their wedding, to which all of illustrious and worldly Paris was invited—their union was not only that of two exquisite creatures but also that of two princely families—they went away to a château in Brittany, near the sea, to hide the first delights of their happiness. The honeymoon lasted a long time! Now they have returned, they are coming back into society; the elegant crowd, happy to see them again, considers them and greets them with tender respect. For their love has its legend, noble and poignant.

It is known that they loved one another for a long time, without being able to admit that they loved one another; that their parents, for reasons of self-interest, did not want to consent to the marriage. Adoring one another, they could have rebelled and fled, but they were honest fiancées who wanted to conserve themselves intact for the nuptial bed. In spite of their despair they had the patience of true passion. And it was by virtue of dolorous

51

resignation and mute prayers that they finally obtained one another.

Because of that legend they are loved and honored. Everyone takes off their hats when they pass by, and sympathetic whispers surround them on all sides. It is wrong to say that Paris is egotistical and frivolous, that it is only interested in scandalous adventures; it is able to render justice to honesty, to sincere love, and to rejoice in recompensed virtues. They, meanwhile, in their slow carriage, are intoxicated by that sweet triumph, conscious of having deserved it, and respond to the greetings with happy smiles.

Jane, however, has suddenly frowned.

"Laure, my darling," she says, "why did you wave your hand at that amazon."

"You don't know her? That's Marguerite de Lizolles, one of my school-friends. We must invite her to our balls."

"Certainly not! Marguerite de Lizolles is one of those women that a woman of your society ought not to receive, ought not even to have known."

"Marguerite? What has she done, then?"

"I don't know whether I ought to tell you—you, so pure and so perfect . . . She's married."

"Well, aren't we married too?"

"Thank Heaven, my sweet angel! But she's married to a man."

"Oh!" said Laure, blushing.

THE THREE HATS

THEY were about to go out. The winter sunlight, traversing the window panes with pale gold, advised the lovers to take a cool stroll in the as-yet-leafless paths where one walks a little rapidly, wrapped up in furs, huddling together, mingling the warm breath of kisses behind the muff.

"I have three hats!" Juliette exclaimed. "Which should I put on?"

"I don't know," said Valentin.

"Would you like me to put on the red hat? On my hair it resembles a large tousled poppy blossoming in wheat."

"No," said Valentin, "not the red one."

"Forgetful! It was the day when I wore it for the first time that I permitted you, for the first time, to lift up the veil that refused you my lips."

"That kiss, cruel woman, only rendered me more bewildered and even more unhappy."

"Would you like me to put on the blue one with pink moss? It's pretty and mischievous, and, slightly tilted over the ear, one might think it were a bouquet laughing loudly."

"No, said Valentin, "not the blue one."

"Ingrate! I wore it, however, on the morning when I sat on your knee, fearful and trembling, in the back of the carriage, in the Bois."

"But you drew away so quickly, cruel woman, because of an officer going past on horseback."

"Ought I, then, to put on the mauve one, with its foliage veined with wine lees, like a vine lead burned by the sun?"

"Yes, yes! That one! I want that one."

"And why?"

"Because . . ."

"Because?" demanded Juliette blushing, as she remembered.

"Because, in the evening of the definitive embrace and the irreparable abandonment, the evening when, going as fast as possible, I had already made of all your silks and lace something torn and scattered that trailed on the carpet, I left you that hat, a vine leaf indeed, which you were wearing on your head."

THÉRÈSE'S CHEMISE

THE extraordinary thing is not that Thérèse had taken off her chemise—everything happens down here, I know, Juliette!—but that she couldn't find it when she wanted to put it on again. Where was it hiding, the fine transparent batiste, imbued with recent perfumes, the supreme veil that had withdrawn for an hour a reliable modesty from the whiteness of her breasts and her perfect legs. Behind the chairs of the little room in the inn—it was in a village in the Pyrenees, almost Spanish, that the two lovers had come together—under the table, under the bed, among the curtains, they searched for the vanished chemise, in vain.

"Can you understand it?" said Thérèse.

He could not understand it either, and they searched every corner, irritated and enraged, for a long time. They remembered that at one moment, in the feigned forgetfulness of kisses, the wind from the mountain, in a fit of jealousy, had broken through the window and rushed into the room, upsetting the furniture, rattling the door, catching light things and fabrics in a whirlwind. Had it carried the chemise away, that wind? Like a great white bird with open wings, had it fled, in a gust, into the night, between the high crags, inflated, crumpled and torn, and was it hooked on to some rocky point, or finally alighted down in the valley, on a low roof of thatch and foliage, perhaps on the steeple of the little new church? Improbable adventures, scarcely possible, for a chemise, in the dark, far from the bed.

Finally Thérèse gave up searching. She was very pretty, her cleavage flattened under the starched short-front, the top of her neck swelling under the tight pressure of the false collar; for her lover, not without the sensation of a more absolute conquest, had offered to replace the vanished garment with a more virile envelope. And they departed, gladly leaving of their happiness, in that distant solitude, what a butterfly leaves of the dust of its wings on a deserted rose-bush.

But how changeable the hearts of women are! The man she had adored, she ceased to love. She scorned the former tenderness, she detested the room in the inn, with the little hard bed, so soft, where the wind of the mountain had come to overflow the curtains. Thérèse, for having heard, only once, the evangelical word of a handsome Dominican, had felt her soul touched by grace. No more balls, no more fêtes, no more tender flirtations after waltzes in the embrasures of windows, where the curtains, without one having anything to do with it, fell appropriately.

Pious, even devoted—with remorse for her past and the vain kisses of yore—she merited being offered as an example to repentant sinners, or those on the brink of repentance. Her director was already permitting her to hope that celestial mercy might discount her former errors, redeemed by a remarkable abstinence. She was more severe toward herself. She did not believe herself entirely purified of former soiling. She imposed penances and fasts upon herself; she demanded the bloody kiss of cilices and the wrath of disciplines. Then the desire came to her to go on a pilgrimage, barefoot, girded with rope, to the little Pyrenean village where she had committed—O remorse!—the sin of lust.

She departed, not on foot, but by the express, not in a woolen robe tightened by a harsh rope, but in a silk dress, semi-mourning, from a good couturier. No matter; she departed. She would lodge in the inn that had been the witness and accomplice of her sin; she would humiliate herself publicly! The idea of a confession before everyone pleased her, as a good punishment from which salvation might be born.

She arrived, she visited the village curé, who approved of the intentions of the penance, but estimated that a public confession would not be devoid of scandal. He proposed another fashion of obtaining divine forgiveness. The church of which he was the servant possessed a marvelous relic that, for two years, had been performing all the miracles imaginable; for having touched it, or merely seen it, the lame ceased to limp, the crippled could whirl their crutches round their heads, the hunchbacked cried: "Who said I had a hump?"

Bewildered, Thérèse wanted to see, touch and kiss the admirable relic that doubtless cured infirmities of the soul as well as those of the body.

"Gladly," said the worthy curé; he took her into the little chapel, where the relic had been placed in a glass case under the monstrance.

"It's certainly from Heaven that it came to us, since it descended in the steeple of the church two years ago, one stormy night, and the delicious immaterial odor with which it is still imbued recommends the conviction that it belonged to the Holy Virgin herself!"

"Oh!" cried Thérèse, kneeling down in ecstasy and piety. Then, with the permission of the curé, she kissed the divine chemise, fervent and certain of pardon, not recognizing the Alençon lace border, nor the embroidered mark, nor the culpable perfume of ancient flannelette . . .

A CASTILIAN ADVENTURE

WITH his hand on the hilt of his sword and the flap of his cloak over his shoulder, Don Manuel, a young cavalier who had come to Madrid to see the celebrations that were being held on the occasion of the baptism of the infant Balthasar, was walking through the streets one night, with the air of a gentleman in search of an adventure of battle or amour, when a lady in a black cloak, and heavily veiled, emerged from a house in hectic light, ran to Don Manuel and said to him:

"If you are, as it seems, a cavalier of noble and loyal family, you will save a principled lady threatened with losing her honor and her life! My husband has just surprised me, almost devoid of clothing, in the home of one of his friends, of whom he is jealous, quite wrongly. I had time to take my cloak and throw myself on to the staircase, but he is pursuing me. At any price, hold him back, for if he catches me, I am disparaged and dead."

"Flee in peace, Señora," Don Manuel replied.

And while the lady drew away, he stood in front of the door, from which it did not take long for a man to emerge, who was in great disorder and a rather bad mood, to judge by the wildness of his gestures and the oaths that he was growling.

"Cavalier," said Don Manuel, after a slow bow of perfect courtesy, "Having arrived in Madrid a few days ago, it is not surprising that I have lost my way in the city, which is as large as it is beautiful. You will, I hope, deign to indicate the Calle de San Bernardino to me, where I have the joy of being awaited by a person who wishes me well, and who promised me this evening, at the Florida, to open her window as soon as her duenna has gone to sleep."

"Let me pass!" cried the other. "You can see that I'm in a hurry!"

"I am no less so than you, since the person who is waiting for me has the most beautiful eyes in the world. But doubtless it is repugnant to you to lend me assistance in an amorous enterprise? I can only praise the delicacy of your sentiments, and I am entirely disposed to link myself in amity with a gentleman of such distinguished virtue. Let us not mention the Calle de San Bernardino again! At least you will be prepared to inform me of the route to some church recommendable by the relics conserved there. I shall gladly spend the night in prayer that I had had the sinful design of consecrating to less austere occupations."

"Go to the Devil! And let me pass!"

"What! Can I not make my devotions or love?"

"By Saint Jago!" said the exasperated husband, "are you making mock of me?"

"In your place," said Don Manuel, "I would have perceived that some time ago."

Then they drew their swords. It was a fine duel, with grating frictions of steel and flashes in the dark: a very long duel, the two combatants being of equal strength and courage.

Certainly, thought Don Manuel, *the veiled woman has had time to reach safety.*

As he completed that thought, his adversary's blade entered beneath his left breast, profoundly, and he fell, his head on the paving stones, with a loud cry.

"God have pity on your soul!" cried the victor, ready to continue on his way.

"One last word," said Don Manuel, gasping. "Is the lady you are pursuing young and beautiful?"

"What does it matter to you?"

"It matters a great deal! I would be desolate to die for some sad old woman with a moustache and rheumy eyes."

"Know, then, that Doña Ana, who is scarcely twenty years old, is the most beautiful woman in Madrid."

"Thank God!" said Don Manuel, rendering his soul.

THE CAGED KISS

HE was amorous, childishly, of that child. He suffered a great deal because of that amour. That was not because she did not love him, but because their parents did not want to consent to their marriage. Once, when he lay in wait for her—it was a little before sunrise when the dawn was hesitating to be born—he saw her, so blonde and so pale, at her window. She gazed at the pale morning sky, he gazed at her, also at first light. Charmed by the nascent gleam, believing that no one could see her, she did something ingenuous and lovely, sending a kiss with her pink fingers to the imminent daylight. At the same time, an awakened bird uttered its call beneath the sky, as if that slight sound were the song of the gesture that she had made.

The amorous young man saw the kiss, heard the voice, pursued the bird through all the branches of the wood, caught it, and took it to his house. Now, he is very happy, for, from morning till evening, always, he can hear his beloved's kiss singing in its cage.

THE ECLOGUE IN THE BOUDOIR

WHEN they had talked long enough about fabrics and compared the merits of famous couturiers, the two socialites, in the bright boudoir of straw-colored silk—for they were both brunettes—where cups of tea were fuming lightly on a lacquered side-table, started talking about their husbands' mistresses.

"Personally," said the Baronne, "I've adapted very well to being deceived by Monsieur de Marcinac. It creates a likeable solitude for me in the evenings, which is entirely to my taste. The best thing about husbands is their absence. But I'm particularly grateful to mine for having chosen a charming woman for a lover."

"It's certain that the fidelity of lovers would be a great embarrassment," said the Comtesse. "We have so many things to do! Visits, dinners, balls, and flirtations too, take up a considerable time. And like you, I'm all the more satisfied in being deceived because Monsieur de Valensole has settled on a choice for which no one can criticize him."

"We've done well," said the Baronne, "to live a very different life from theirs; between us and those whose names we bear there is a residue of solidarity, thanks to which we have our part in their successes and defeats, their pleasures and their pains, and we would blush, not only for them but for ourselves, if they were to abandon themselves to unworthy amours."

"The tenderness we gave them in the beginning," said the Comtesse, "we have not taken back entirely; what they have conserved of it mingles with the quantity of personal tenderness that they can dispose in favor of others, and we would be somewhat humiliated if anything of us were debased in unrecommendable liaisons."

"Thank Heaven" said the Baronne, "I have nothing of that sort to fear. Of a noble family, almost princely, my husband's mistress occupies a very illustrious place in our society, and everyone pronounces with respect the name that he murmurs amorously."

"I am as proud as you," said the Comtesse, "for other reasons. No princess, my husband's mistress! An operetta diva, but very famous, acclaimed and adored; it's for her that Emperors come from Brazil and princes from England."

"Her beauty is divine!" said the Baronne. "Tall, pale, blonde, as if transparent, like a walking dream."

"Her grace is diabolical!" said the Comtesse. "Petite, utterly charming and dainty, with dimples in her cheeks, her breasts and arms, like a doll of pink flesh."

"Her elegance is incomparable," said the Baronne. "She draws the pomp of long dresses with a slow majesty, and it's on her regal forehead that the diamonds gleam that she has deigned to accept from my husband."

"Scant elegance but utterly chic!" said the Comtesse. "With a scrap of crumpled lace, she's bizarrely exquisite; her short skirt has frightening flights, and no man can glimpse without the peril of losing his head the anklet of peals that my husband has given her."

"And truly, she loves him," said the Baronne, "since, widowed for two years, she has refused, in order not to quit Monsieur de Marcinac, the hand of a reigning Duke in one of the German lands."

"And truly," said the Comtesse, "she's faithful to him, for I'm assured that for six months no one else has supped with Monsieur de Valensole in the private rooms of Vois or the Maison-Dorée."

Thus the two worldly beauties conversed in the straw-colored silk boudoir, where the cups of tea were fuming lightly on the lacquer side-table; and they both felt moved to pity—a scornful and laughing pity—for poor Madame Ruremonde, whose husband, they are assured, is the lover of a bourgeois woman who is not very pretty, in whose house bingo is played on Wednesdays, and for poor Madame Lurcy-Sevi, whose husband is in love with the fat Constance Chaput of the Bouffes, who has such big feet!

THE TALKING IMAGE

FOR want of a mirror, the little dryad Amymone was not sure of being pretty. The infant goddess had certainly perceived that the fauns were disturbed by her and watched her through the branches, and that the flowers leaned toward her with a tender languor, and that, among the leaves of her tree, the nightingales sang more amorously than in other trees; but the fauns might have had bad taste, the flowers might only have been inclining in the wind, and the nightingales might have been unaware of the beauty of nymphs.

Once, leaving the forest, she paused on the edge of a rock and looked at herself in the water of the sea, which, under the blue sky, shone as smoothly and brightly there as the water of a tranquil lake. She made a gesture of astonishment and chagrin. What, she was that ugly! That was her hair, those green strands, as damp and oily as seaweed? That was her mouth, that broad mouth with large teeth, and her skin, that skin the color of sealskin, and her ear, that ear bristling with grass, like an enormous seashell? But the young marine god who was laughing through the water raised his head, steaming with foam, out of the water.

"What you can see is my face," he said, "not your face; and if you want to know what you are, beautiful dryad, you'll have to come closer and look at yourself in my eyes!"

THE EIDERDOWN

BECAUSE of the eiderdown, they have a big quarrel that evening, with caresses and laughter, the little wife and the young husband. With hot blood burning in his veins and his neck swelling, he is quite breathless under the envelopment of the duvet, and would like to cast it off, but she, in her chilly modesty, wraps herself up in it and clings to it with her ten obstinate fingers.

"It's so heavy!"

"No, very light!"

"I'm stifling!"

"I'm shivering!"

And there are long debates amid the amusing anger, almost a struggle, in which happy arms enlace, and the squeals of unexpected tickling, and the reconciliation of the kiss. O sweet combats of the conjugal bed, when the honeymoon still rises delightfully in the cloud of the curtains on the horizon of the alcove! Finally, the little wife triumphs, and, under the caressant heaviness she goes to sleep slowly, only her nose outside the covers.

Is she asleep? The husband follows her project. Gradually, carefully refraining from laughing for fear that she might wake up, he lifts the eiderdown and pulls it, makes it slide, pushes it, and watches it spread over the carpet in a soft fall. It's done! He breathes deeply.

But she will doubtless shiver with cold, the sensitive sleeper, and unclose an eyelid, and complain? No, not at all. Although the eiderdown is no longer on the bed, she feels a warmth dress her entire body with delights; her mouth expands in a smile of infinite wellbeing, in which her lovely teeth are gleaming; and, gently oppressed, without opening her eyes, in a dream, she says:

"It's true, though, that it's heavy, and a little stifling."

A ROMANTIC ADVENTURE

B Y HERCULES, said Valentin, the adventure has nothing chimerical about it. Once, before dawn, I descended from a balcony. It was by means of a silken ladder, naturally. Having set foot on the ground I was blowing a few kisses toward the shutter, which was ajar, when my back encountered the back of a man who, walking backwards, was addressing a final gesture of salutation to a half-closed window from which was hanging, quivering in the air, a silken ladder.

"Eh!" I exclaimed. "Who are you?"

"Abbé Desiderio," the man replied. "And you?"

"Raphael Garuci. Where are you coming from?"

"My lioness's room. And you?"

"Pauper's blood! My lioness's room."

"Is she pretty?"

"A redhead. And yours?"

"A redhead. Why are you leaving at dawn?"

"She's jealous, and giving me a headache. But why are you leaving so early?"

"Christ's blood! For exactly the same reasons as you."

"Abbé?"

"What?"

"The ladders are still dangling along the walls."

"So what?"

"The darkness is still thick, and you can bet that in closed rooms, no one can see a thing."

"So?"

"It's not easy in the dark to distinguish one man from another. Do you love your mistress?"

"Not much. And you?"

"Not at all. Abbé, I have a whim to go and see whether your beauty has skin as soft as mine."

"Raphael Garuci, your beauty might perhaps have softer skin, but I'd swear that she doesn't have longer hair, and I'd like to be sure."

"It's settled!"

"It's agreed."

"One more thing, Abbé. Can two good gentlemen exchange mistresses like this without swords emerging from sheaths and a little blood emerging from the body? What do you think, Abbé?"

"I think, Raphael, that it will be necessary for us to cut one another's throats."

"Agreed!"

"Settled! Where are you lodging?"

"At the hostelry of that wine-sack Palforio, by the Pope's mule. And you?"

"The same, by Saint Peter's fat."

"See you soon, then."

"See you soon."

And I headed toward the right, while he went to the left.

He stopped.

"Raphael!" he exclaimed. "Your memory's failing, and you're playing your role poorly."

"Why?"

"You've forgotten to give me your cloak."

"That's true; take it."

"Thank you."

"Yours?"

"Here it is."

"Thank you."

He scaled my mistress's balcony, thanks to the silken ladder, and, thanks to the silken ladder, I reached the window of his.

"Good luck, Abbé!"

"Garuci, good luck!"

MENDICANT AMOUR

ALTHOUGH she was the daughter of the foremost bailiff in Melun, Mademoiselle Brigitte was not loved, having stupid eyes that squinted, a mouth devoid of smiles and gestures devoid of grace; and she did not love, because she had no heart. But the god Amour took pity on Mademoiselle Brigitte and swore by the cleavage of his mother Cypris that she would possess everything that she lacked for experiencing and inspiring tenderness.

With a blindfold over his eyes, carrying a placard suspended around his neck that read *Blind for having gazed too much at the beauty of young women*, he established himself as a mendicant—a mendicant clad in purple and precious stones!—at the door of the emporia of the Louvre, and held out his golden bowl to the Parisiennes who were entering and exiting in a rustle of adorable dresses. From one he requested the gaze that has the color of promised paradises; from another, the mysterious smile of Giocondas, which charms and drives to despair; from another, the omnipotent grace by which a piece of tulle gives the impression of lace woven by fays and given the thinnest arm the slow curve of a swan's neck.

As Parisiennes are unable to say no to Amour, they filled his bowl quite willingly, and he took those precious alms to the bailiff's daughter.

Now Mademoiselle Brigitte is loved, having vague troubled eyes that disturb, and a divine cruel smile, and grace; but she does not love yet, because she has no heart. That is not because the god Amour, begging at the door of the emporia of the Louvre, had neglected to ask for the inestimable alms, without which everything is worthless, from the Parisiennes who were entering and exiting with a rustle of adorable dresses, but the Parisiennes were not able to give him a heart, because they have never had one.

ENCOUNTER

EARLY in the morning—not yet midday—the Comte went into his wife's room. Was it true that the previous evening, as she was going up the staircase of the Comédie-Française, she had given Monsieur de Puyroche a slap? The anecdote had run around the club last night, but he had refrained carefully from believing it.

"You were quite wrong! I certainly did slap that Monsieur."

Yes, with her little gloved hand, on both cheeks, and very well. *Flic! Flac!* Everyone had heard it.

"Do you know, Madame, that de Puyroche, in all probability, will demand a reckoning from me?"

"Well, Monsieur, you will kill him."

He smiled, sat down beside her, and started talking to her, very amicably. Come on, she would confide in him, she would explain things to him. He would like nothing better than to fight. A duel is no big deal. But it was still necessary for him to know the whole story. He did not want, at any price, to be ridiculous. Why had she slapped the young man? Yes, why?

"You're absolutely determined to know?"

"Absolutely."

She told him everything. She had learned that Monsieur de Puyroche, over dessert, at dinners in male company, had said very nasty things about Madame d'Argelès, affirming, among other absurd things, that the poor young woman in question, being fearfully thin, was obliged to have recourse, in order to pad out her bosom reasonably, to the most vulgar artifices.

"I could not tolerate anyone spreading such a rumor about my best friend, and, having found myself face to face with Monsieur de Puyroche . . ."

The Comte had stood up, wrath in his eyes.

"I shall kill de Puyroche!"

"I certainly hope so."

"He's a calumniator!"

"Brazen."

"Madame d'Argelès is not thin at all!"

"Quite the contrary."

"Admirably made!"

"That's my opinion."

"The full and firm cleavage of a living statue!"

"Snow molded in two cups, which doesn't melt."

They fell silent and looked at one another. They both had the same question on their lips. But they were people of good taste, who burst out laughing. And after advising her husband not to spare Monsieur de Puyroche, the Comtesse merely added, laughing more loudly: "See how one finds things out, though."

THE RECOMPENSED LOVER

"I admire you! What do you want?"

"Oh, almost nothing—everything!" she replied.

"That's very little."

"That's my opinion."

"But can you not, sweet angel, specify your desires?"

"Can you not divine them? First of all, I want all the flowers of summer and all the stars of the night. That's the least you can offer me as an opening move."

"Exactly. I've put them for you, all the stars, in this collection of sonnets, and all the flowers, in this book of rondeaux."

"I also desire humbler things."

"Speak quickly, dear soul."

"A house in the Parc Monceau, built by Garnier on the plan of the house of Diomedes and furnished by Penon after the apartments of Madame de Pompadour."

"You shall have it."

"The colonnettes of the threshold will be pink jade, and the silks of all the furnishings will have been selected by me alone in the silkworm factories of Taicoun."

"That goes without saying."

"I want twelve Russian horses, so handsome that none similar have ever been seen stepping in the princely pathways."

"I'll buy the ones that were harnessed to the imperial carriage on the day of the tsar's coronation."

"All the dresses, naturally, and all the hats!"

"You'll have limitless credit at Monsieur Puck, who has established himself as a costumer in the Avenue de l'Opéra, and Madame Titania, who is about to open a fashion boutique in the Rue du Quatre-Septembre."

"A few jewels too, and a few precious stones."

"All Golconda in earrings, with Ophir in necklaces and Visapour in bracelets."

"In addition, as it would please me to be loved by a man of genius, you will make arrangements to write, as quickly as possible, a certain number of masterpieces."

"Tomorrow I shall send to the printer a poem more sublime than *Eviradnus*, and I shall have a drama staged at the Odéon more beautiful than *Formosa*."[1]

"As it might be, on the contrary, that I shall one day have the whim to see you infamous forever, it's necessary for you to give me a bank draft on which you have imitated perfectly the signature of Alphonse de Rothschild."

"That's a mere bagatelle."

"I shall also demand other sacrifices."

"Command!"

"You have somewhere, I'm told, a legitimate wife, with two or three children, and also a poor aged mother whose sole support you are?"

"That's true."

---

1 *Eviradnus* is a section in Victor Hugo's *La Legende des siècles*, added to the 1859 edition. *Formosa* (1869) is a drama by Dion Bouci-cault.

"You'll give me the pleasure of throwing out your wife and children . . ."

"They'll be picked up in the street as vagabonds."

". . . And no longer paying any heed to your mother."

"The old woman will die of starvation. You don't want anything more, my sweet angel?"

"Nothing, for the moment. However, as one never knows what might happen and I have a horror of poverty, you'll doubtless judge it appropriate to assure me an inalienable annual income of two hundred thousand francs."

"Not more?"

"No, that will be sufficient."

"And when I've offered you the flowers and the stars, the house and the horses, the adornments and the gems, my glory and my dishonor, and my abandoned wife and my dead mother, what shall I have in exchange for all that, dear heart?"

"The pleasure," she said, "of having given it to me."

ACCORDING TO A PANEL

POWDERED, with her cheek reddened by rouge—
one might think it snow on a poppy—a beauty spot
on her breast, a beauty spot at the corner of the eye, and
all beribboned with madly floating favors, Phillis has led
her flock into the shade: the innocent lambs around her,
bleating, deliver themselves to a thousand games in the
long grass, from which the butterflies scatter; and the
shepherdess, sitting on the edge of a stream amid the bil-
lows of her inflated skirt, dips one of her bare feet in the
water, so small and pink, giving the impression of a little
bird drinking.

She is quite convinced that no one will be able to
surprise her in that solitude. But Tirsis, in violet silk, is
watching her from the branches, and he suddenly shows
himself, animated by the most ardent furies of amour.
In vain she invokes Diana, who defends the modesty of
shepherdesses. Diana, with her unkempt nymphs, passes
in the distance without hearing her, in the excitement of
the hunt, while the lover, skillful in seizing the opportu-
nity, tears the satin of her bodice and kisses the satin of
her skin.

Well, if the divinities are deaf, Phillis will summon
men to her side. "Stop, Tirsis, stop," she murmurs, "or I'll

shout for help, and someone will come, and will punish you, as befits a reckless shepherd."

He takes no account of threats or pleas. He cries out in a resounding voice: "I adore you, most beautiful of shepherdesses," while pushing insolence to the extreme limits.

And Phillis says: "Shut up! Be quiet! Oh, Tirsis, what if someone heard you!"

THE INDISCREET INDIVIDUAL

IN the black and pink room, a pretty backcloth for whiteness, Madame de Ruremonde is presently at the point in her toilette when one takes between the teeth the chemise that is about to fall, while another chemise awaits, folded, on the armchair. One minute—less than a minute, the time to appear and disappear, like a naiad at the surface of the water, in the crystal of the cheval-glass—and the beautiful young woman will be naked! Already she has unclenched her teeth, opened her lips slightly, and the Malines is about to slide . . .

But Madame de Ruremonde utters a cry of fright—the cry of a frightened swallow—and, with her mouth, her hands and her arms, retains the chemise. By the sound of breathing behind the door, she has divined that someone is spying on her! Yes, certainly, there, in the drawing room, a man has put his eye to the keyhole, in anticipation of the moment of exquisite nudity. It's frightful. And Clementine has just taken away the peignoir.

What can she do? Ring? Call for help? Yes, right away. She is about to pull the bell cord. However, she wonders. Who can possibly be there, watching her? Baptiste, perhaps? She utters a mute laugh. In which a great deal of pity is mingled with some scorn. It's true, yes, that they are to be pitied, these poor valets de chambre. They live in the cruel proximity of the wife, of all her graces and perfumes. Baptistes? No, Tantaluses. It must be exceedingly painful, at length.

Certainly, one cannot, under any pretext, admit the culpable condescensions for which the devil on two sticks reproached more than one socialite. Fie! The wretches! Can one imagine such an extravagance? But after all, without taking things to the extreme, one might perhaps, from time to time, without doing it expressly, by chance, give a little furtive consolation to those poor wretches. A drop of water, for Tantalus, is a great deal. Where would be the harm if a bodice too lightly fastened, or a chemise too rapidly dropped . . .

No, it isn't Baptiste who is observing through the keyhole. He has gone out to take a commission to the couturier's. The neighbors' son, perhaps? A schoolboy of fourteen, with furnaces in his eyes, who always slips into Madame de Ruremonde's apartment on days of leave to purloin novels from the bookcase. It's not extraordinary that those children seem to take pleasure in gazing at women; they are taught so many things; in Ovid or Virgil, smiling and semi-naked, under oleanders or behind willows, Venuses are asleep or Galateas are fleeing. Mythology gives them ideas. Are the long dresses and sleeveless arms of fantasias that one enjoys in matinees sufficient to realize the dreams of those young men? For they are men—my God, yes! What an ecstasy it would be for them suddenly to recognize, fully, in a delightful unclad woman, the living chimera of the Immortals!

It might also be the case that Clementine has let in a visitor without warning her—she is so scatterbrained, that Clementine—some madrigal-singing roquentin, or one of those stupid and conceited fops who pay court to her with words from the stable. Madame de Ruremonde laughs wholeheartedly. What an amusing barbarity, appropriate to redouble the rage of disappointment, perfect and unforgettable.

Oh, damn it, too bad. Baptiste, the schoolboy or Monsieur de Puyroche, she is in a hurry; it's necessary to get dressed. Anyway, she might be mistaken. She does not ring; she lets the lace escape her teeth and, a statue of luminous snow, raising her arms, she stands up in front of the cheval-glass for a long time, untroubled, in her generous immodesty.

But suddenly, she shudders, and, gripped by shame, she goes pink from head to toe, and she flees, envelops herself in the curtains of the bed, and shouts, in alarm: "It's horrible!" For she has realized, by the sound of a cough in the drawing room, that the indiscreet individual behind the door is her husband.

THE GOOD DRINKER

"PERSONALLY," said John Knickerbocker, burger of London, as stout as a vaudeville innkeeper, with a nose clotted with bleeding rubies, "I can say that there isn't a gentleman in old England, nor on the continent, who can boast of having seen me roll under the table. Gin, brandy, porter and ale have never triumphed over me. When I've prepared a bed of good roast meat and cheese, a river of half-and-half can flow through me without inconveniencing me in the slightest. My capacity is incomparable. I absorb and I contain immeasurably. If you were to puncture my belly, what would emerge would slake the thirst of all the drunkards in Dublin for an entire Sunday.

"There are only two persons in whom I recognize faculties worthy of praise, from the viewpoint of the ingestion of liquids, and that's my colleague Anaximander Ponnoner, a moderately good ale-drinker, and Mrs. Flora Knickerbocker, my wife, truly remarkable where brandy is concerned. I hold them in esteem, but I had to pity them one day when they pushed audacity so far as to want to measure themselves against me. Scarcely had they emptied, him thirty quart-pots of beer, and her four bottles of eau-de-vie, than they fell under the table, together, in one another's arms.

"All night long, still drinking, fresh, fit and imperturbable, I had the chagrin of hearing them utter melancholy sighs, so uncomfortable were they, and heart-rending plaints, which they mingled with kisses and caresses, like people who do not have a head on them. And the next morning—truly, I was beginning to get thirsty— they were still so drunk that one would have had all the difficulty in the world making them understand the inconvenience that there would have been, on my part, in letting both of them lie in the same bed."

THE RAT

IN the cameo drawing room, into which the open window let the odor of roses, amid the scattered clothing, ribbons, tresses and hair-clips, they are grouped, tying knots, all the beauties of the epoch, exhaling an air of amber and emitting a cloud of powder with every shake of the head; all the disappeared lovelies that Edmond and Jules de Goncourt have revived in an unforgettable book: Madame de Choiseul, still slightly melancholy about the "passionette" that she had for the darling musician Louis; Madame d'Arty, who sups at Guimard's and gladly recounts the "jolly horrors" of petty houses; and the extravagant Madame de Stainville, still smitten with Clairval, who is ruining her and beats her; and Lady Sarah Lennox, sister of the Duke of Richmond, the most beautiful cleavage in the world; and Madame d'Epinay, who has never forgotten what she overheard one evening over champagne: "Modesty? A fine virtue, that one attaches to oneself with pins." And Madame la Marquise de Lignolles, who fought a duel the previous week with the Comtesse de Gèvres over Michu of the Comédie Italienne; and others still, chatting and laughing amid the silks and muslins, while the little abbé, in a corner, is leafing through a new pamphlet that the hawker has just brought, and humming: *For a kiss collected from the lips of Iris.*

But suddenly, there is a cry: "A rat!"[1]

Yes, a rat, climbed in from the garden, or come from the servants' parlor. It has been seen, it has crossed the room; not very large, but frightening nevertheless. Where is it?

They get up, they try to flee. There is a pell-mell of fearful dresses, a flutter of little screams. A rat is quite capable of slipping under a skirt and climbing up the legs!

Madame de Stainville affirms that she felt it passing between her heels.

"I think it leapt on to my chair!" cries the Comtesse de Gèvres, half-swooning.

Madame de Choiseul advises her to call for the cat.

"Aiee! It bit me!" says Madame d'Arty.

"Where?" asks the Abbé.

And Lady Sarah Lennox, all a-tremble, has lost her head to the extent of opening her bodice to see whether the rat might be hiding between her two breasts of snow and roses.

And the fear continues to increase; there is hubbub of disorder, a tumult of panic.

"Do you think it's poisonous, Abbé?"

Only the Marquise de Lignolles has remained seated, imperturbably. She is a courageous woman who, before

---

1 It might not be irrelevant to the symbolism of this story that *le rat* [the rat] was one of the slang terms employed in nineteenth-century France for syphilis.

adoring Michu, had no fear, so it is said, of confronting the brutal tenderness of two ruffians of valets, one German and the other Champenois. She bends down unhurriedly and, dragging the rat from beneath her skirt, which was caught in a mousetrap of lace, she says: "That's a lot of noise for such a little beast, and it seems to me that we've seen many others."

JULIETTE AT THE WINDOW

FOR two long hours now—in the clear spring night, through which breezes pass—that Juliette, in the verdure of the casement, has been awaiting her good friend, straightening her curls, neck bent, her eyes alert, her nose tilted back like a pink convolvulus.

She has heard numerous cabs going along the street, with a rattle of wheels that made her heart beat faster; they did not stop outside her door. A single carriage, by virtue of the cruel pity of chance, came to a halt. *Him! It's surely him!* No, it was the tenant on the third floor, a fat monsieur whose nose is so red that it pierces the darkness like an ember.

Juliette has also listened, ardently, for the sound of footsteps on the causeway of the boulevard, in the silence of the deserted quarter. More than once she has thought she recognized . . . no, the man who turned the street corner was a municipal coachman, with a white waxed canvas hat, on foot, whip in hand, or some drunkard beating the wall.

She is finally enraged, stamping her heel, tapping the window resoundingly with angry little fingernails. All evening, she has had a heart so full of the most ardent tenderness, and spring gives her amour such lovely advice! For two pins she would weep, the abandoned woman, but one does not see tears reddening the edges of her eyes needlessly. She slams the window shut. Too bad! He can come or not come; it's all the same to her; she won't wait any longer.

She prowls around the room, undoes her hair, unfastens her bodice, puts a book on the night-table beside the lamp—a book that she will read, alas!—lets her skirt fall, unbuttons her ankle-boots, slides off her stockings, and in the rustle of a chemise, buries herself between the sheets, the sheets of the empty bed, the cold bed, the pillow of which she plumps up with blows of her fists, furiously.

But scarcely has she lain down than she hears the sound of a key turning in a lock, a door opens, and another . . .

Him! And Juliette, who puts on a semblance of being asleep, huddled at the side of the bed, tells herself with a little laugh that, in fact, the best means of making a belated guest arrive is to sit down at table.

THE LITTLE FAUN

A T the bend in the path, on his terracotta pedes-
tal, the little faun was laughing boldly. Horned,
swollen-cheeked and pot-bellied, he laughed, the lubricious, naked young god—being the one who presided
over the fluttering couplings of sparrows in the sand, the
crepitant caresses of dragonflies over the heather, the rapid and fleeting marriages of squirrels along the branches.
But it was not sufficient for his triumph to show that
bestial joy. Brazen to the point of cynicism, disdainful
of all modesty, like a drunken Eros, he affirmed in broad
daylight, like a sign of supremacy, his arrogant virility, like
a young king holding the scepter of command. With the
result that the faun in question was an object of scandal
for the honest passers-by, and that many strollers could
not see him without blushing beneath the eyelashes or
concealing a little laugh behind the rosy trellis of their
interlaced fingers.

But she, Berthe-Marie, the demoiselle of the château, charitable and devoted, so good and so pure, who
went every day to the church where people pray and the
cottages where alms are distributed, passed by without
blushing or averting her eyes from the bold simulacrum;
she considered it, smiling, with a complacency that was
slightly astonishing but not at all fearful, in the peace

of an inviolate innocence, neither pensive nor anxious, the depths of her blue eyes reflecting the perfect ingenuousness of a child taking pleasure in looking closely at the pictures in a missal, and touching them with her fingertips. For she was candor itself, ineffably ignorant of evil; and if lakes of immaculate azure exist on some Alpine plateau, which have never even been traversed by the shadow of a white cloud, it is one of those lakes that her soul resembled.

One morning, she went into the woods with her lover, who was her fiancé. Yes, with her lover. Why not? Virgin hearts have their affections too; one can give oneself without giving oneself, and a betrothal ring is not the ring of Hans Carvel.[1]

He almost as young as her, as naïve and tremulous as one another, it was to be an exquisite day! They did not hold hands, were careful not to allow their elbows to touch, both aware as if by instinct of their sensitivity. But their souls were united in spite of their bodily separation.

Wordlessly, they exchanged thoughts in immaterial conversation, the alternating distichs of an angelic eclogue. It was in vain that around them, in the sunlit

---

1 The story of Hans Carvel seems to have been first committed to print in a collection of lewd tales, *Liber Facietarum*, by the papal secretary Poggio Bracciolini (1380-1459); it was retold by Rabelais and than recast as a fable in verse by Jean de la Fontaine. Carvel, an old doctor with a young wife, dreams that the devil gives him a ring that will prevent him from being cuckolded as long as he wears it. When he wakes up he finds that his finger is stuck in her vagina, with the result that "Hans Carvel's ring" became a common euphemism for that anatomical feature.

air where ardent odors were vaporized, branches brushed one another with gentle caresses, and flying green-gold beetles traced redoubtable magic circles, and the voice of the nightingale faded away, ecstatically, beside its nest, and that the entire wood, full of love, enveloped them, gave them the culpable advice of embraces and united lips; they went through the perils, without paying any heed to such sweet wicked temptations.

Not once—not once!—did he press her to his heart, not once did they look at one another too closely, sighing. They were, in that paradise which they did not want to lose, like an Eve and an Adam who were not thinking about forbidden fruit. Yes, such would be, all day long, the slow excursion beneath the trees of those two pure children, and I would even swear that they would not linger to search in the moss for the little fresh strawberries that are reminiscent of kisses, nor to interrogate the daisies, those providers of troubling answers.

It was after dark, in the moonlight, when they returned. Certainly, in the depths of her large blue eyes, Berthe-Marie still had—and why should she no longer have had?—the ingenuousness of ineffable ignorance . . .

When they passed before the faun, horned, swollen-cheeked and pot-bellied, who was even more boldly triumphant, the lubricious little god, like a young king holding the scepter of command, she turned her head very swiftly, and started to laugh, stifling her laughter in her friend's neck.

THE PROMPT GIRL

T HE honest grandmother began by giving the little prodigal a couple of slaps. Then, while the girl shed hot tears, as red as a poppy, with her fists in her eyes, she gave her a remarkable speech.

So it was true! There was nothing to tell my good friend, or, rather, yes, that was precisely what there was to tell, since she had a lover! She admitted it, she dared to admit it! A lover. At sixteen! With her little modest air, with her eyes always lowered—truly, one would have given her to the good God without confession—she was at that point of debauchery and cynicism. One would have thought that she had nothing in her head but her doll or her Japanese baby. Oh, well yes, the doll that pleased the demoiselle was a man. What shame! Fie! She ought to go back underground. What? She, who had received such good principles, who had had in her family, the example of all the virtues, had committed such a frightful sin! It must be, in truth, that she had the devil in her body.

But what exasperated the honest grandmother most of all was that Louisette had succeeded in deceiving the surveillance exercised over her.

"For, in sum, I can say that I've guarded you well, night and day! In the three years that you've been here, you've only been out on your own twice. The first time was a week ago, for five minutes, to buy needles and thread, the second, the day before yesterday, for an hour, to go see your aunt in Batignolles, who is ill. One hour was sufficient for you to become a good-for-nothing! The most foolish wait for someone to pay court to them, they resist for a month, six months or a year. You were in a hurry! Oh, wretch, in an hour, you have . . ."

But the girl, weeping more copiously, said: "No, Grandma, you're mistaken. It wasn't that time, it was the other . . ."

THE GOOD AUNT

MADAME AMÉDINE DE TRÉNIS—Aunt Amédine, as she was called—wrapped herself up, comfortably and cozily, in the sheets embroidered with English stitch. She was on the brink of going to sleep, with a little smile of satisfaction on her lips. She had reason to be delighted. During the day, Madame de Trénis had married off her niece, whom she adored, and things really had gone very well. How many people at the church! All Paris—the Paris that counts. Talazac had sung like an angel. Now the married couple were alone, on the second floor of the house, in the nuptial chamber.

Oh, certainly Jane would be happy. In spite of his excessively tall stature and somewhat heavy build—reminiscent of a robust manual laborer—Monsieur de Cardan, young, with blue eyes and black hair, was a very handsome fellow, and was reputed to be as gallant a man as could be.

"Ha ha! Happy—perhaps she already is?"

Aunt Amédine thought of those things complaisantly, in the profound soft bed that was warming her up. What concurred in putting her in a good mod, preparing her for pleasant dreams, was that she had played her entirely personal part in the success of the day. At thirty-six one is not old, especially when one is pale and for paleness she feared no one, not even her niece, whose pallor was not as soft, a trifle too cold. Jane was snow—"Me, I'm cream"—with the consequence that, during the ceremony, not all gazes had been for the bride, and, in the sacristy, a young man had said in passing, in a low voice, the slightly brutal but not shocking words: "In truth, I'd be well content with the aunt!" He was not disgusted!

There was more than one who thought like him. For example, she had often noticed that Monsieur de Cardan himself—a fiancé, almost a husband!—did not look at her without some pleasure. Those men! Let's see! Thank heaven, though, she had recovered from all follies. Widowed five years ago, having taken her family duties seriously, she was far from having ridiculous ideas, even after Jane's marriage, and the most amorous man in the world, even if he had Monsieur de Cardan's blue eyes and black hair . . .

"Aunt! Aunt Amédine! Aunt!"

The door resounded with little blows of a fist, rapid and redoubled, which gave the impression of beating a drum.

Madame de Trénis leapt out of bed and opened the door, and the new bride, in the disorder of fear and flight, her hair undone, the sleeve of her peignoir flapping, threw her arms around her aunt's neck, with tears in her eyes, stammering . . .

It was frightful! Monsieur de Cardan . . . Oh, God, if one knew . . . Utterly frightful . . . But she would stay here, she would hide here. Oh, certainly, she wouldn't return to her husband. And it was necessary to lock the door, to barricade it with all the furniture . . .

At first, Aunt Amédine had a strong desire to laugh. These innocents, how easily it frightens them! However, when she saw that Jane did not calm down, still sobbing, refusing energetically to go back up to the nuptial chamber, she became serious. She remembered stories that she had been told. New husbands sometimes have cruel brutalities, either because the ardor of their passion carries them away, or because . . .

Her duty, as the head of the family, ordered her to discover the truth. She wrapped herself in a plush dressing gown, which brought out the whiteness of her neck and chin, and went out, saying to her niece, gravely: "Wait for me. I'll go talk to your husband."

Half an hour later, though, when she came back down, she was not grave at all. It was with a smile in her eyes and on her lips that she said to the young bride, still full of fear: "Go on, little girl, return to your husband, child."

Then, as Jane was still hesitant, not wanting to go away, Aunt Amédine added: "He has furnished me with all the desirable explanations, and I swear to you that the wrongs are all on your side."

THE WINDOW DISPLAY[1]

LOOK. The shop-window is sparkling in the sunlight, and a hundred little portraits appear behind the clear shiny glass. There are archbishops and princes, generals and magistrates, tenors and young women. The men are rather ugly; the young women, for the most part, are not beautiful but they have low necklines; they compensate for their plainness by showing more. One, too fat, sitting astride a chair, is smoking a cigarette and, leaning forward and overflowing the back; another is raising her arms and yawning, like a woman who wants to be relieved of boredom. This one, who has no robe, is, fortunately, wearing a solid breastplate; that one is wearing nothing at all. Sometimes, one sees Adah Menken in a bathing costume, on a rock.[2] The poor woman, now a skeleton, is still showing her legs. Death itself has to be able to extract her from ignominy. This is as lugubrious as a violated sepulcher, as a rightfully lifted shroud. But there it is! It is a sale of photographs, of which it is necessary to dispose.

---

1 This is the meaning of *l'étal* that is implied by the scene described in the story, but it is by no means irrelevant that the same word is commonly used to refer to a butcher's meat-stall.
2 The American actress Adah Menken (1835-1868) was the highest-paid actress of her era, notorious for having appeared on stage in *Mazeppa* apparently nude, riding a horse. She died in Paris.

In front of the window there is a crowd. Idlers with empty heads, in quest of a thought, pause there. A schoolboy who has just relighted his cigar in a nearby tobacconist's, stands on tiptoe and contemplates, open-mouthed, blinking. When he goes away he will take with him in his memory the wherewithal to illustrate by night the deadly pages of some stolen book. Sometimes, a thin young man in a frayed jacket, without a winter overcoat, halts in front of the shop and looks for a long time, sadly, at all those young women, which, he, poor devil, finds beautiful, and whom he will never have, since one pays them. Then he draws away, hastening his steps, for the time to be back in the office has already passed. Today, he will work poorly, and tonight he will have bad dreams. Do you know what anguish, in a man vowed to hopeless poverty, can be engendered by desire alone?

A respectable Monsieur mingles with the group. He is forty or fifty years old; he is dressed in a correct fashion. His entire attitude indicates clearly that he has not come here expressly, that he is just passing, or waiting for someone who has arranged to meet him at the street corner. It is not him who will screw up his eyes, like the crowd of idlers that surrounds him. The gaze with which he scans the window is perfectly indifferent, detached; if anything can be read therein it is a slight scorn, even disgust. Sometimes, however, his eyelids blink energetically, showing and hiding by turns a gleam in a yellow eye. But that does not last long. His smile is accentuated in a grimace that evidently means: "Pooh! What horror!" And he turns away, still looking out of the corner of his eye.

Then, arm in arm, laughing and chattering, young women arrive, emerging from a workshop or a coming from a department store. You know them well. They are the ones that one encounters in the street at lunch time, in twos or threes, bare-headed, noses in the air, with a ribbon knotted round the neck, their crumpled Orléans dresses showing a gray lining at the rips in the elbows and the poorly-buttoned bodice pierced in more than one place by the black tip of a whalebone. They arrive, they push, elbowing their way through, laughing in people's faces, and in two seconds they are in the front rank, their foreheads stuck to the window. They do not limit themselves to looking; they comment on the types and the poses. They are familiar with matters of photography. Like young men of letters who, in order to put on airs, salute illustrious men who pass by, calling them by name, they say in loud voices; "Look, there's Blanche!" or "Look, it's Alice!" With that, they go away, as they came, laughing and chattering, pulling one another, and their carelessness resembles impudence. The respectable monsieur draws away at the same time. One could easily believe that he were following them, if he did not have such a respectable appearance.

Whenever there is a stereoscope, a queue forms. Among merchants of photographs the stereoscope is what the chamber of horrors is at Madame Tussaud's; that which is slightly hidden must be more interesting. Certain insatiable spectators occupy the conquered position for such a long time that there is often impatience, and even quarrels. At other times, eyes succeed eyes rapidly, like travelers at a ticket-window; you can imagine the disappointment of a man who, after waiting for a good ten minutes, sees the towers of Notre-Dame instead of Mademoiselle Raymonde's legs, and the dome of the Invalides instead of Mademoiselle Desclauzas' shoulders.[1] Yesterday, while I was observing the shop window, I noticed a stereoscope from which people were standing aside very rapidly, with the most surprised expression.

It's some monument, I said to myself, and had a look. It was not a monument. It was the Medici Venus.

"That's strange; the Venus is naked, and much more naked than the demoiselles her neighbors."

I had doubtless spoken aloud, for one of my friends, who was passing, having understood, put his hand on my shoulder, and said: "Yes, she's naked, of course—but she's beautiful!"

---

1 The second actress cited is Marie Desclauzas (1841-1912); the surname Raymonde was not uncommon in the Parisian theater, but none of the contemporary actresses employing that name acquired lasting fame.

AT A FAST GALLOP

BY NIGHT, on the mountainside, on the descending route, amid a torrential noise of breaking branches and rolling stones, the lover and the mistress are fleeing at a fast gallop, recklessly. And in the breathlessness of speed, they do not stop talking.

"They'll catch up with us," he says.

"It'll be all over for us," she says.

"If they kill us, so much the better!"

"Oh, yes, yes, if they kill us!"

"But no, they won't kill us."

"Why not?"

"They know that living without you . . ."

"Oh, despair . . . !"

"Would be crueler for me than dying with you . . ."

"Oh, to die together!"

"And your husband will spare us . . ."

"Alas!"

"You, because he loves you . . ."

"I abhor him!"

"And me, because he hates me."

They fall silent in the increased pace of their flight.

"You're certain," she resumes, "that no hope remains to us?"

"Not one."

"No refuge?"

"Not one."

"And we'll live without seeing one another again?"

"Never."

"Well then, let's die!"

"Ah! I want that!" he cries.

"Listen. At the bottom of this path . . ."

"The precipice opens, enormous and frightful."

"Dig in the spurs!"

"Yes."

"Faster! Faster still!"

"Yes."

"And let's both fall . . ."

"After your last kiss?"

"Here it is!"

"Into death!"

Then the lover's horse launches itself into the gulf. But she, a skillful Amazon, with a violent tug on the bridle, has stopped her mount dead on the brink of the abyss, its limbs trembling. Leaning forward beneath the stars, she watches, with a smile, the man tumbling from rock to rock, holding out his lacerated arms to her.

THE THREE DRAWERS

WITH a resolute gesture, like a person who will no longer change her mind from now on, Madeline designated the Japanese cupboard with three drawers, the pink and gold lacquer of which the glare of the lamplight caused to tremble, and very gravely, the darling young woman said:

"Open one of those three drawers—and try to choose well, Valentin, for in each of them, I've hidden a response to the plea that you haven't ceased addressing to me for six months. If you put your hand on the tender response—the one that says yes—it will be necessary for me to consent not to refuse you. But dread encountering one of the harsh responses; you'll never see me again!"

"Alas," he says, "the odds are two to one against me. What cruel thought has occurred to you, dear soul?"

"Oh," she said, "I shall have the consolation, if I have to oblige you, of being able to blame my sin on chance."

He hesitated for a long time between the three drawers. His tremulous hand went from one to another, not daring to pull the little gilded ring, and his heart was constricted by the fear of a bad choice. He finally decided, his eyes closed, counting on the divine mercy of providence.

O joy! O infinite delight! The response—a sheet of pink paper, so rapidly unfolded—bore the adorable word: *Yes*.

He took Madeline in his delighted arms and carried her away, blushing all over. No resistance was possible now—save for an odious breaking of the promise given. And the Comtesse was an honest person who took pride in honoring her engagements. She resigned herself. Until the hour when they gray and rosy fingers of the morning parted the muslin of the curtains, there was the cherished tenderness of amour, which calms down and is always reanimated.

"Oh," she asked, astonished, "what do you need now? Of what do you have to complain, dear ingrate?"

"I have a worry," he said.

"You! Next to me? What?"

"I have you due to chance, not of your own accord."

And he remained thoughtful.

But she burst out laughing.

"Idiot" she cried. "It was the same response that I put in all three drawers!"

GOOD INFORMATION

WHEN the Marquise de Portalègre and Madame de Ruremonde sat down in the little mauve drawing room, there was an exchange of light perfumes between the two costumes—visiting clothes on the one hand, almost a peignoir on the other—and they looked at one another, prettily.

"Have I arrived too early?" said the Marquise. "Please excuse me. It's a matter of some urgency, and I won't keep you long."

"In what way can I be agreeable to you, Madame?"

"I've come in search of information."

"Ah! About Clementine, yes? A very decent girl, and very adroit. Above all, a good hairdresser. Then again, not curious or talkative. It was in a fit of temper that I dismissed her. Certainly, you'd do well to take her, and I miss her already."

The Marquise de Portalègre laughed behind her half-veil.

"It's not a matter of your chambermaid."

"Oh! What is it about, then?"

"Monsieur de Marciac."

"Monsieur de Marciac?"

"Of course. You're astonished Why? Isn't my step quite simple? What! The most imprudent people, before taking on a coachman, a cook or a groom, ask for serious references, make enquiries, demand certificates, and, when we're on the point of admitting a man into our intimacy—which is always equally serious, in sum—we shouldn't judge it appropriate to obtain information from well-informed persons?"

"Oh! You're on the point . . ."

"And you're so well-informed. Look, let's understand one another quickly and not waste any time. I confess to you that Monsieur de Marciac doesn't displease me. He's not too handsome—being beautiful is ridiculous for a man—he has fine manners, speaks with distinction and dresses very elegantly. In sum, he doesn't inspire any repugnance in me. You know the moment when it only requires something trivial for everything to be settled? That's the moment I've reached. But before engaging myself in a definitive fashion, I wanted to see you. It's said in low voices that Monsieur de Marciac has been your friend for quite a long time, and you won't refuse, I imagine, to enlighten me a little on his account, and even give me some advice?"

"In truth," said Madame de Ruremonde, bursting into laughter, "if you absolutely insist . . . First of all, you know that he's married?"

"Yes, yes, he told me. A very simple woman, who lives in retreat, not inconvenient. One can pass over that?"

"For myself, I haven't had to complain about her."

"Good."

"The person of whom it's necessary to be suspicious is little Anatoline Meyer of the Bouffes. Monsieur de Marciac has never managed to detach himself from her completely. He goes two, three or four months without seeing her, and then, if he recognizes her one evening at a première, in the chorus of an operetta, there he is, caught again! It appears that the little one is quite extraordinary."

"Extraordinary . . . in what way?"

"He won't fail to tell you. He has a mania for talking about her."

"That's very impertinent!"

"But so amusing! You'll see. In any case, Monsieur de Marciac has the wherewithal to enable that inconvenience to be forgotten. He is, in truth, a perfectly gallant man."

"Discreet?"

"As appropriate. Not too much, not too little. He compromises, and doesn't cling. That's a nuance."

"Certainly. Not quarrelsome? Not jealous?"

"No, no. On the contrary, very accommodating. Up to date with things: admitting flirtations, understanding perfectly well that even the most beautiful amours aren't eternal, and that a woman has to think about the future."

"That's perfect."

"Rich, too, with fine relations, a relative of two ministers. He sometimes gets very precious tips about variations in the value of shares. That's a consideration. Our husbands are so miserly, since the crash!"

"Alas! But there's one important point that you haven't mentioned. Is Monsieur de Marciac . . . affectionate?"

"How do you mean?"

"I won't hide it from you that, under my frivolous exterior, I'm something of a dreamer—melancholy, even.

I've always had the desire to encounter a soul smitten with the ideal, like me."

"Aiee! Love of the ideal isn't Monsieur de Marciac's dominant quality. But on the other hand . . ."

"Ah! Truly, on the other hand . . . ?"

"All that one can imagine."

"It's necessary, then, that I resign myself. In sum, the information isn't bad, on the whole."

The Marquise de Portalègre had risen to her feet. "But I was forgetting the principal thing," she added. "How long did Monsieur de Marciac remain . . . ?"

"In my service? For three years, I think."

"That's what makes up my mind completely. I have a horror of change."

"What? You intend to keep him for that long?"

"Longer, if I can."

"Oh, then it's necessary that I give you one last item of information. If you want Monsieur de Marciac . . ."

Madame de Ruremonde leaned toward the visitor and whispered in her ear, very quietly. What did she say? They burst out laughing.

Finally, on the doorstep, the Marquise said: "It only remains for me to thank you, Madame."

"Don't mention it, Madame?"

"But it's a matter of one good turn deserves another, isn't it?"

THE DEVOTEE

THE veil lowered to the chin did not prevent me from recognizing her. It was Madame Belvélize, for sure. Who else could have that pretty pink smile and those tender blue eyes, which put a rose and two cornflowers beneath the veil? Besides which, the Belvélize arms were on the door of the coupé. She got down very quickly, in a rustle of faille in which there was a hint of jet, said to the footman: "Let the carriage wait!" and went up the steps of the church of Saint-Roch almost at a run, with a brisk click of heels on the stone.

I was entirely edified. That fervent socialite at a church was a fine thing! Getting up at nine o'clock in the morning after some ball to come and make her devotions, yes indeed! She was not one of those who imagine that, in order to be saved, it is sufficient to have loved a great deal. Love—the best form of charity—is not reprehensible in itself, but it is appropriate to add a little prayer to it. After the boudoir, the confessional. After one has been clement, implore clemency. And the good God refrains carefully from refusing anything to someone who does not refuse very much.

Thinking that, I was going back and forth outside the church, and was in no hurry to continue on my way. What retained me was the hope of seeing Madame de Belvélize again shortly, when she got back into the carriage. She's so lovely to look at! And a little of her perfume, like an invisible flower, came to my nostrils: a subtle, almost culpable perfume, sanctified by incense.

Half an hour went by, the time of a low mass. I was increasingly edified! Madame de Belvélize had nothing in common with those silly devotees who expedite affairs of religion as rapidly as possible, thinking, while their pretty nose is buried in a missal, that if the officiant doesn't hurry, they'll miss the appointment with the dressmaker. No, she practiced, austerely and entirely; and, since she was not reappearing, it was because she hadn't restricted herself to hearing the mass. She was confessing; there was no doubt about it.

Oh, to be, for a few minutes, the fortunate director of conscience to whom she was relating, with joined hands, the small sins of her flirtations and the grave, but more charming, sin of kisses poorly refused. Was he able to interrogate her, at least? How I would have insisted, in his place, while delicate aromas rose through the grille, on the smallest detail of the confession, how I would have demanded, as a pitiless casuist, that she reveal to me scrupulously all the circumstances of the abandonment: the place—boudoir or bedroom—the time—perhaps midnight—and whether she had bare arms or whether the peignoir, by an unfortunate hazard, might not have yawned a that precise moment!

But I repelled those guilty thoughts. I was wrong to abandon myself to such imaginings, while Madame de Belvélize was accomplishing her Christian duties. It was, in truth, lacking respect for her.

More than an hour passed! I was full of admiration for such a perfect fervor. While I was pacing back and forth, she was humiliating herself before the priest, weeping over her errors, demanding penances, not finding herself sufficiently punished, finding Heaven too merciful. Saintly little soul! Who would have believed it? I promised myself not to leave anyone unaware of the devotion she hid so carefully. Her virtue would be known. And those who willingly said malevolent things would be obliged to shut up.

Two entire hours had gone by when Madame de Belvélize reappeared! I was not mistaken: she must have been confessing on her knees and weeping, because her faille dress, with the hint of jet, was crumpled, and the redness of wiped tears colored the corners of her eyes, as if there were a rose petal around each cornflower.

In the legitimate excess of my veneration, while the penitent ran down the steps, I was about to approach her and compliment her humbly on her sacred zeal, when it occurred to me—oh, the evil thought!—that the church of Saint Roch has more than one door.

INGENUOUSNESS

EULALIE BISQUET, more commonly known as Lila Bisquet, is a little actress who rides like Penthesilea, but everyone agrees in saying that her stupidity is truly remarkable. More foolish than Agnes, although long since enlightened, her imbecility is perfect, devoid of innocence: she would be capable of believing that infants are made by the ear . . . and she did, once.

It is Lila Bisquet who played the role of Nigaudina in the last fantasy play at the Théâtre du Châtelet, and not one pretty girl—pretty she is, adorably, with her narrow mouth with full red lips—would have been able to play the role as well as her, since it consisted of crossing the stage, in the first tableau, on a winged tarasque, and for the rest of the play showing a bewildered smile of irremediable stupidity. Furthermore, she showed her thighs; no one held that against her.

Because of her legs, in fact, and her fine equestrian audacity, the director of the social circus, that has millionaires for gymnasts and gentlemen for clowns, proposed that she take part in one of the hippic and acrobatic performances that he offers to clubmen and beautiful women of his acquaintance. She was very flattered and swollen with pride, although, being pampered, she had no need of that augmentation. When she was told that she would have to ride a horse bareback, however, she seemed troubled and amazed. She looked at the people with pretty frightened and delightfully stupid eyes.

No, for sure, she would not do what was asked of her; she would never dare, for a start. Other exercises, she would gladly do, but not that one. Oh, it was impossible, that one. In order to convince her it was necessary to insist for a long time, to assure her that she would have a great success, to repeat to her that there was nothing difficult about it, that it would be child's play for an equestrian as skillful and courageous as her.

"Since you wish it!" she finally said, resigned, with a thoughtful expression.

The evening of the performance arrived. A full house: all the sportsmen and all the affectionate women. Monsieur de Verdelis launched himself from one trapeze to the other with the stolen temerity of a Léotard. Cannonballs and weights were placed on the Comte de Valensole's shoulders that would have made Atlas say: "Not so heavy!" And Monsieur de Puyroche, striped like an Auriol, made quips that would have made the most melancholy victim of spleen roar with laughter.

Then, when a black stallion had been led out, without a bridle, bit or saddle, Lila Bisquet, throwing off with a single gesture the large cloak that enveloped her, appeared in the ring, in the full glare of the gaslight, with no species of garment or veil—not, not even the hypocritical transparency of batiste—and leapt on to the horse, all snow and roses.

Lila Bisquet, the angel, had understood the requirement as "Ride a horse *in the nude*." But no one protested, for it was a divine spectacle, that beautiful girl extended, without clothing, so white, on the gleaming black coat of the galloping horse, her hair mingling with the mane.

GOLDEN FROTH

IN the convent of which Mazet de Lamporecchio was the worthy gardener,[1] but before he had gardened—I mean, in the time of initial innocence—the rumor spread one day, without anyone knowing where from, that a man was hiding under the habit of one of the nuns. One of those angels was a devil! One of those ewes was a wolf! I shall leave you to imagine the alarm.

There was no talk of anything else in the refectory, in the chapel and the pathways of the orchard. There were blushes, tremors, everyone walked with the desire to recoil, to flee, as in a wood where it is known that there is a large beast. A man: that was frightful. Even the most intimate friends looked at one another suspiciously. "Who can tell? Perhaps she's the man!" The sister who carried the water became an object of general horror because she had a moustache.

But the one who was the most tormented of all was a young novice, scarcely thirteen years old, whose name was Sister Ninetta. Her eyes red, as if she had been weeping, striking her breast continually as if in remorse for some great sin, she could not hold still, and uttered deep

---

1 The convent gardener Mazet de Lamporecchio is featured in a story in Boccaccio's *Decameron* that formed the basis of one of Jean de La Fontaine's *nouvelles* in verse.

sighs. If anyone asked her: "What's the matter, Ninetta?" she fled very rapidly, without a word, as if she were carrying away some terrible secret.

Finally, one day, after having remained in her cell all morning, she went to find the superior and said to her, head bowed and trembling, with poppies in her cheeks: "You know, Mother, that there's a man in the convent?"

"I know that it's rumored, but I don't believe it."

"Oh, Mother, you're quite wrong not to believe it. It's only too true that one of the nuns isn't what she appears to be."

"What! Have you acquired proof . . . ?"

"Alas, yes," said Ninetta, her head in her hands.

The good abbess, anxious, was also astonished. Ninette was then as perfect a virgin as could be; having entered the convent very young she had only just reached the age when little girls become young women, and one could say that she had never seen any other men than Saint Joseph with the long beard and the Evangelists, also bearded, painted in the chapel. How could it be imagined that, utterly innocent, she had discovered something that had escaped more subtle and better-informed gazes?

"Explain yourself, Ninetta. The person you think might be a man is . . . ?"

"It's me, Mother!" cried the novice, dissolving in tears.

At those words, the superior, as one might imagine, was greatly reassured.

"In truth? It's you?" she said.

"Me, alas."

"Well, Sister Ninetta, how did you perceive that?"

"I'll never dare say it aloud."

"It's necessary that you whisper it, then."

Then Sister Ninetta, having drawn nearer, whispered in her ear, always blushing redder, for a long, long time, saying things such that the abbess finally could not hold back any longer, and burst into laughter, holding her sides.

Then tapping her on the cheek, she said: "Come on, little one, stop worrying, and believe that you're not a man just because you have a little frothy golden down on your chin!"

JULIETTE'S BREAST

THAT evening, in the ground-floor box at the Odéon, where she and he were chatting in low voices, very close together, the mad, irresistible desire took hold of him to see and to kiss Juliette's breast. Oh, how natural it was, that desire, since all the perfumes of all the flowers of the fields, wild hyacinths, lilies of the valley, narcissi, those innocences which smell so sweet—and also the odors of less virginal flowers; lilies, carnations, gardenias, those heady sensualities—were emanating, O young breast from your warm snow!

Juliette was annoyed at first, raising the objection of the nearby lights and indiscreet gazes; but he insisted with such tender prayers, the depths of the box were so obscure, that she ceased to say no, the good girl. And for an instant, in the dark corner, he had been caressing with his eyes and his lips the dear embalmed whiteness, when the usherette opened the door and said: "The people in the next box are asking you not to keep a bouquet in your box, because the odor is going to their heads."

THE ACTOR

WHEN he returns to his apartment after the theater, the handsome pale actor with the profile of a young Roman cannot help smiling, accustomed as he is to such homages, at the extent to which all the furniture in the drawing room is cluttered by marvelous flowers: enormous heaps of gardenias, sumptuous bunches of irises, and a huge basket of white roses collapsing in a cascade of snow. On wreaths of carnations, forget-me-nots form the letters of his name, and here and there, little bouquets of violets—two-sou bouquets, the offering of a humble devotion—mingle their discreet prayers with the frantic desires of magnificent florescences. He smiles, not astonished—for he is the one who troubles all the women, and does not deign to be troubled himself.

As soon as he comes on stage—a seigneur in white satin illuminated with gold, or a gentleman clad in almost black cloth—a shiver of ease and desire rises, dress by dress from the ground-floor proscenium to the third gallery, because of his slimness, simultaneously delicate and robust, his brown eyes, in which a dream is floating, his lips, like a woman's mouth, and his beautiful hands, slightly elongated, at which he gazes while speaking. In the boxes, the fans of socialites quicken, refreshing blushes, scattering the warmth of exhalations. The footstools tip over under the nervous tapping of ankle-boots. The heavy breathing of fat bourgeois women in the balcony inflates the silk of corsages as if to make them burst like balloons over-filled with gas. And up above, the young seamstresses suck imaginary kisses in the acidic sugar of mandarin oranges.

He does not seem to pay any heed to the emotion he causes: no understanding gaze, no gesture of thanks. He triumphs as if unaware of it; to the pride of being victorious he adds the pride of disdaining his victory. He is tranquil, with a hint of coldness. In order that no female spectator can appropriate the passionate transports of the role for herself, it is in a very composed voice that he says: "I adore you," to the amorous woman in the play, still gazing at his beautiful long hands.

Off stage, he is no less indifferent. He never responds to the enthusiastic love letters that are hidden in the bouquets, as perfumed as the flowers; he does not even read them any longer, forgetting them, seals intact, on his dressing-table, between the pot of white greasepaint and the hare's foot.

The door of his dressing-room and that of his apartment are closed to all supplications; the dressers and domestics have severe orders: "Flowers, yes; women, no," he said, one day, while he was making the pink nacre of his fingernails shine with the aid of a cat-skin. In vain the Marquise de Portalègre has been waiting for him every evening for three months in her coupé outside the artiste's entrance. In vain Madame de Lurcy-Sevi has sent him a tortoiseshell casket filed with fine pearls, writing: *There are not enough pearls in the world to send you as many as*

I have shed tears. And truly, also, that exquisite creature, all blonde and tanned with gold, a Brazilian blonde, the Baronne de Villabianca, who leans her exceedingly low neckline in which her breasts are oranges, over the edge of the proscenium, has sworn that she will infallibly kill herself if she does not obtain the favor of a conversation with him. He has remained insensible, the handsome pale actor; and this evening, again, he considers without softening the tenderness of the supplicant flowers that clutter the drawing room.

As he goes into his bedroom, however, he stops, because of a sound, and turns round. From the basket of white roses, overturned and rolling, a woman has just emerged, quivering, all warm gold, through the batiste of her chemise. It is the Baronne de Villabianca.

He looks at her without surprise. "What do you desire, Madame?"

"You," she says, putting her naked arms around his neck.

But with his long hands, so lovely, with the bright nails, he rejects the seductive effrontery of that caress.

"All I can do for you, Madame, is not to beg you to go out at this undue hour, in this bad weather."

With that, he goes into his bedroom and locks the door behind him.

The Baronne, who is very cold, not knowing where to clothe herself, picks up the basket, nestles within it, and shivers until morning in her chemise, amid the roses.

THE INNOCENT

S HE said to her friend:
    "Have I deceived Ludovic? I don't know. Decide.
I'll be quite content if I haven't deceived him. I went to
his apartment that evening, my dear, I swear to you that
I went to his apartment. I ring; the door doesn't open. He
must have fallen asleep while waiting for me. But I have
a key. I open the door, I go in. There I am, groping my
way, into the bedroom. 'Ludovic! Ludovic! It's me!' No
reply. I think: *How soundly he sleeps!* And I amuse myself
imagining his surprise when I wake him up by tugging
his beard. It doesn't take very long to take off a hat, a skirt
and stockings. I slide into the bed, shivering . . . My dear!
A shaven chin! And while two vigorous arms enlace me,
and a mouth closes my lips, I think fearfully that I must
have mistaken the first floor for the second! Now, tell me,
have I deceived him?"

"Not in the least," replies the friend. "There's no sin
without evil intention."

"Oh, how glad I am! But, after having recognized my
error, perhaps I should have run away?"

"And make a noise? That would have been to act like
an idiot."

"Oh, how much pleasure you're giving me. But perhaps I ought to have removed myself by remaining totally
insensible in the arms of that unknown man?"

"In order to cause him distress? In order for there to be a scene, a scandal? You acted very honestly in not annoying him unduly."

"Oh, how you're consoling me! But perhaps I ought not, in the following days, to have stopped in the apartment of the first-floor neighbor?"

"Why? Not having ceased to be innocent, it was certainly your right to continue to be in the same fashion."

"Oh how I thank you! For, you see, I'd have died of chagrin if I'd deceived Ludovic."

THE GOOD EATER

DURING his last sojourn in Warsaw, the pianist Golvinat received from Princess Saratoff an invitation to supper. He was slightly perplexed. Should he accept or refuse? Certainly, robust and colossal in stature, endowed by nature with a stomach difficult to sate, he ordinarily felt sure of himself; but the princess was reputed to be a frenzied eater, an incomparable devourer of the heaviest victuals, and she had never yet encountered a guest capable of matching her. That supper would be a duel!

At the prospect of measuring himself against such an adversary, he hesitated. The desire for victory finally prevailed over the dread of defeat. After having prepared for the contest by two days of appropriate abstinence, he responded to the princess's invitation without too much anxiety, determined to make supreme efforts.

She was waiting, already sitting in front of a table laden with dishes and bottles.

As soon as he saw her, he was entirely reassured.

As young as eglantines, as slender as trembling reeds, and so pale, perhaps consumptive—Ophelia, in truth—Princess Saratoff would already be sated by the second course. Come on, people had exaggerated things; he would triumph easily.

The meal commenced almost without words.

Ophelia, yes, but Gargamelle! Everything, everything, fish, meat, game, the vegetables dreaded by the prudent eater, and also heavy pâtés, she swallowed, swallowed, swallowed everything. Astonished, he was not afraid. It was no longer a time for hesitation. It was necessary to vanquish or die. He put on an extraordinary performance. For three hours—without changing his plate; the princess did not give him time—he engulfed as much food as it would have required to nourish half an army on campaign for an entire day. At one point he paused, but, seeing that she was still eating, he recommenced furiously. And in his mouth, the slices of salmon, the slices of ham, the slices of pâté, the chicken thighs and the pheasant wings were like the dead leaves that a swirling storm wind accumulated in a hole.

He was finally obliged to stop, sated, and he looked at the princess, sure of his victory.

Her eyes were full of tender admiration. He swelled with pride. It was certain: he was triumphant!

But then, while he panted, inflated, enormous, unable to do any more, she got up, opened a door, and showed her guest, in another room, another table overladen with a frightful abundance of victuals, and then, drawing the frightened guest toward the white tablecloth as if toward the curtains of an alcove, she said, smiling: "Now let's have supper."

THE QUESTIONNAIRE

WITH his hat on his head and his stick in his hand, ready to leave, Sylvère d'Espagnac, after a last glance in the mirror—a handsome chap, in truth!—rang for his valet de chambre and asked, with certain emotion:

"The forename, Justin?"

"Clarisse, Monsieur,"

"The name?"

"Madame de Villerose."

"Title?"

"Baronne."

"Age?"

"Barely twenty-three."

"Married?"

"Believed to be a widow."

"The house?"

"17 Rue de Penthièvre."

"The floor?"

"The second, above the entresol."

"Let's recapitulate. Baronne Clarisse de Villerose, aged twenty-three, widow, resident at 17 Rue de Penthièvre, on the second floor, above the entresol?"

"Yes, Monsieur."

"Good. Oh, Justin, get the trunks ready, for if the Baronne consents, I'll leave for Italy with her this evening,"

With that, Sylvère d'Espagnac traversed the ante-chamber, went down the stairs and climbed into his carriage, after having said to the coachman: "17 Rue de Penthevière, quickly."

For three years, every morning, at the same time, a similar scene, almost identical, had been reproduced inevitably.

To his master's questions, without the aid of any memory or any information, without using any strata-gem, Justin had to riposte with the forename, name, title, age and address of a complete imaginary woman, and Sylvère had never failed to go to the designated domicile, any more than he had failed to be dolorously moved when the concierge replied, quite naturally: "I don't know that person at all."

Why that seemingly absurd comedy? Because, weary of facile amours and the foreseen of life, Sylvère d'Espagnac only wanted henceforth to owe the woman with whom he would fall in love to the most extraordinary hazard.

Did he really hope that a mysterious accord between the will of Providence and the imagination of his valet de chambre would permit him, some day, to encounter the predestined mistress or wife?

Yes!

And that dream was all the dearer to him because it was perfectly chimerical.

Neither the beautiful young women who never re-fused, nor the beautiful socialites who sometimes consented could deflect him from his unique thought; more than one, among those that others coveted madly, had given him in vain the gaze or the smile, the vague and tender signal that does not forbid approach.

One sole desire! Only one!

It was with ever renewed anguish that, every morning, he had himself taken to the address indicated by the inexhaustible fantasy of a romantic valet.

The carriage stopped. As he went through the coaching entrance, Sylvère trembled involuntarily, walking slowly, in order to delay the moment of the cruel response that was, alas, all too familiar.

"Madame de Villerose, please?"

"She is at home, Monsieur."

"What!" he exclaimed, his heart leaping. "No, you misheard me: I said: Madame de Villerose."

"Well, yes."

"Baronne Clarisse de Villerose?"

"Exactly."

"A young woman of about twenty-three?"

"I believe so, yes."

"Who is widowed?"

"For two years."

"And who lodges on the second floor?"

"Above the entresol."

He hurtled forward, ran up the stairs four at a time, did not have himself announced, pushed one door, then another, went into the boudoir, and fell breathless at the feet of a stupefied young woman.

As she was blonde and delightfully pretty—hazard had carefully refrained from stopping on such a fine road—not for an instant did he have the idea of getting up again.

What words did he pronounce? With what irresistible passion did he reveal, not without combining voice and gesture, his bold hopes? I don't know. Madame de Villerose, to whom he doubtless did not fail to relate in some detail the story of his realized chimera, perhaps understood that it would have been madness not to submit with a good grace, and to the end, to the fatality of such an astonishing coincidence. Perhaps she was one of those women who ordinarily do not put up much resistance to the kneeling supplications of young men. The incontestable fact is that the trunks were not packed in vain that day.

Sylvère and Clarisse knew dear, slow excursions in a gondola in Venice, under the azure immensity, and the delight, in Naples, of holding one another in an embrace on the balcony in the evening, while the flames of Vesuvius rose up in sheaves toward the stars. More infatuated with every passing day, Sylvère was perfectly happy, and he only had a very fleeting sadness on the morning when Clarisse said to him:

"Return to France? As you wish, my sweet master. But you'll sack Justin, won't you? Oh, with a good sum. I'd be very embarrassed, you see, and couldn't help blushing in the presence of that poor fellow, since he was an accomplice to the ruse that I imagined, for love of you, my friend."

POOR AMOUR

TO buy that bouquet, the poor devil in love with the beautiful actress had gone to the office without breakfast for a month, sold his black suit, sold his few books, pawned the only mattress from his iron bed, borrowed from all his comrades, and renounced soup and dessert absolutely at all his dinners at the Quatre-Marmites in the Rue Lamartine. If, already then, he had become, because of sleepless nights and reduced meals, even thinner, it did not matter. He had been able to buy the bouquet: a hundred-and-fifty-franc bouquet!—"They don't make any more beautiful," the florist had told him—and have it taken, for ten francs more, to the dressing room of the actress by the theater concierge.

Now, the magnificent roses, in full bloom, like the mouths of beautiful giants, were flourishing in the adolescent's presence.

Every evening, for three days, he came to the theater and asked whether there was any response. Oh, he had not limited himself to sending flowers; he had put a letter under the roses, a mad, hectic, sincere letter in which all his desires were exaggerated, all his desperation sobbed. The first evening, when the concierge responded to him: "No reply," he was not astonished. The beautiful young woman had not had time to write, even a word. The second evening, nothing again. Still nothing, on the third.

He went away head bowed, with a desire to weep. What! She had not taken pity on him? She had not been moved by the story of so much suffering, so many devoted prayers? He asked for so little, though. A few words: "I feel sorry for you," or "Don't die." How cruel she was to him, poor fellow.

As he went up the Rue des Martyrs he thought about his cold room, his bed, now so hard, devoid of a mattress, his ever solitary bed. But no, no, she must be as good as she was beautiful. She had not replied today, she would reply tomorrow. Certainly, she would write to him. Two or three merciful lines, perhaps. With what grateful tenderness he would cover with kisses the dear perfumed letter. Yes, yes, tomorrow. It was necessary not to despair. Oh, he had no regret for having sold his clothes, for having borrowed, for having gone hungry, being so poor, and being so thin, since he would have, thanks to the purchased roses, the incomparable joy of being consoled by her!

As he was about to cross the exterior boulevard, a flower-seller emerged from a brasserie, one of the women who offer at the tables in cafés and the doors of cabs flowers resold at a low price by the concierges or dressers at small theaters. He uttered a cry.

Faded, crumpled and sad, he recognized his bouquet and bought it—his last franc!—and under a street light, his hands trembling and his eyes full of tears, he rediscovered the letter that she had not read beneath the roses that she had not respired.

THE CORONET

B Y what caprice did the Girl with the Golden Eyes, that evening, want the Baron to put on, over the beribboned chemise, the guipure peignoir that fluffed up like light froth, while she put on her lover's clothes? Oh, the subtle and crazy supper so close to the alcove. The waist caught in the tight black frock-coat, the plastron with three implausibly swollen diamonds, the straight collar rising all the way to her dainty ears, she sliced, poured, attacked, full of laughter, with virile impatience, the feminized guest who feigned modesties, and it was the pink lips, where not even a down quivered, that stole kisses from the moustache.

But all of a sudden, there were raps on the door, and Louisette's words through the door: "Madame, Madame! All is lost; Monsieur has arrived. The carriage is stopping outside the door. The time to climb four flights of steps, and he'll be here!"

For there were still—in the nineteenth century!—husbands who conserved the detestable custom of unexpected returns. In vain, many of them had been warned by unfortunate experience of the inconveniences that such conduct almost always produces; that does not prevent certain spouses from persevering in it, and there is a good number of men, very intelligent from other points of view—men of the world, incapable, as they say, of putting their foot in it—who take it into their heads to put the key in the lock of the conjugal dwelling when they are believed to be two or three hundred leagues away. Are they in for it? Very probably, and it's only what they deserve.

However, the Baron and his beautiful friend, in spite of a very natural disturbance, did not lose their heads. In the blink of an eye, while the chambermaid took away the supper table, they had changed their clothes, he resuming the frock-coat, the waistcoat, the trousers, and she donning again, with a tremulous haste, all the lace and ribbons. "Now escape by the service stairway!"

And when the husband came into the bedroom he had reason to be fully satisfied—I could have wished him a worse adventure!—because, in the silent gloom, in which the glimmer of a lamp was dying, not far from the intact bed, in a peace of innocence and faithful patience, the young woman clad in a guipure peignoir that fluffed up like light froth was lying on a chaise longue, her eyes closed, her hand dangling over a book that she had dropped, drowsily.

"You, Fabrice! You!" she said, with a yawn that became the prettiest of smiles. "What a nice surprise! But come closer, Monsieur. Have I aged, then during that long absence, to the extent of being quite ugly, and you don't want to kiss me?"

He kissed her, with all the tenderness possible for a husband. What suspicions could he have maintained before that solitude, that slumber and that seductive awakening? Oh, certainly, she was the most virtuous and the most amorous of wives. As he knelt before the chaise longue she caressed his hair and his beard, kissed his eyelids, said sweet things to him: that she had suffered a great deal during his voyage, that she had stayed at home all the time, no balls, no theaters, obtaining no pleasure from pleasures without him, that her only consolation had been the thought of his return. She was happy herself, almost sincerely, in the joy of the peril averted, in the triumph of her hypocrisy; and with a surge of passion that was only partly feigned, she took her husband's head in her hands and hid it in her bosom, under the lace of the peignoir.

"Ah!" he said, putting his hand to his cheek, where the pink zigzag of a scratch ran.

She went very pale, having understood. One can't think of everything, alas. She had taken off the trousers, the waistcoat, the frock-coat, but not the shirt with the hard plastron ornamented with three diamonds, and now the husband, still on his knees, was considering with eyes widened by a doubtless legitimate amazement the flap of fine cloth on which was embroidered a Baron's coronet.

PIERRE AND PIERRETTE

HANDS full of perfumed bunches of eglantines and pimpernels, the two children were coming back from the woods, She was sixteen, he fifteen; they were so ingenuous, the young lovers—Pierre most of all, but Pierrette too, in spite of the sixteen years at which curiosities awaken and instinctive expectations are disturbed—that they had collected all those flowers that morning, and not a single kiss. And they were coming back delighted, slightly troubled in her case—why, she did not know; perhaps astonished that nothing happens except making bouquets and looking out for warblers when one goes to the woods with one's good friend.

Suddenly, Pierre made a gesture of alarm. Oh my God! There was no longer any means of getting over the water. The wind, with a sudden gust, or some practical joker, with a kick, had pushed the plank of fir-wood that spanned the stream, and the frail bridge had doubtless fled with the current. There was a boat, but it was tied to one of the willows on the other bank.

A very grave situation! Pierre's parents, and Pierrette's, who lived in the little white and green house over there, had strictly forbidden them to go for walks together on their own, and there would be a terrible scolding if the children did not get back unperceived, through the back door, before lunch time.

Could they make a detour and reach the village along the main road? It was necessary not to think of that, because time was pressing. Could they cross the stream, which was not very deep, by wading? Yes, but how would they explain their wet clothing when they arrived?

Pierrette was desolate, weeping over her hands full of flowers. Pierre paced back and forth on the bank angrily, stamping his feet.

Suddenly, he cried: "I've got an idea!"

"What idea?" she asked.

"I'll strip naked, make a package of my clothes, wade through the stream to the boat on the other bank, get dressed again, and come back to fetch you in the boat."

"Oh," she said, blushing to the roots of her hair. "Would you dare to strip naked in front of me?"

The objection was not serious.

"You can close your eyes or go behind that big tree."

"It's true that I wouldn't be able to see you," she said.

As soon as it was agreed, it was done. Pierre, in a few seconds, had taken off his jacket, waistcoat, trousers and shirt, and, lifting his rolled-up clothes over his head, he entered the stream courageously, while Pierrette, who had judged it unnecessary to go behind the big tree, kept her eyes tightly closed. His back turned, he walked slowly, because of the current, in the direction of the boat.

Through the transparent water, green and sunlit, which came up to his loins, he appeared, slim although already robust, and pale, chubby although a trifle frail.

But believe that Pierrette refrained from considering that spectacle, inappropriate for a girl!

Far from cheating, as one does in a game of blind man's buff, she kept her eyelids together with such force that her pretty pink face was wrinkled like a little apple, and she was so sure of herself, so certain of not being tempted by any culpable curiosity, that she did not find any inconvenience in saying, when he reached the middle of the stream:

"You know, Pierre, since I'm not looking, you can walk backwards if that's more comfortable for you."

*N*OW, readers, after fifty stories, I won't add another page to these frivolous pages, and Fantasy is already suggesting other tales to me, when your chambermaid knocks on the door and says: "Does Madame want to get out of the bath?" The work that I thought worthy of being riffled through by your pretty damp fingers, the work that ought to have been, like your reverie itself and continuing it without distraction, softly vague, a trifle sad, and so tender, worldly, certainly, and also poetic, perverse at times, since you are very subtle, more often chaste, because you are, indeed, chaste, and always amorous, which ought to have mingled with languorous stories a few foolish ones, for the water of the bath, shaken by your laughter, makes a pretty splash against the cracked roseate faience or the snowy alabaster; this work—so small but so exquisite—I have not been able to perfect. Such as I have narrated them, however, have you read them, O delightful Parisiennes, the vain vignettes? Will a few of the bright droplets—pearls for having touched you, tears for having quit you—that you scatter as you spring out of the water fall upon the book?

Alas, in the little room decorated with flowery silk or gilded mats, near the bathtub from which a mist of aromas that is like the vaporization of your tenderized flesh still emanates, the book might perhaps be there, but, while the plush of towels caresses you before the fortunate mirror, the author will not.

A PARTIAL LIST OF SNUGGLY BOOKS

CPSIA information can be obtained
at www.ICGtesting.com
Printed in the USA
FSHW010758190319
56469FS

9 781943 813889